# CAMERA LAKE

# CAMERA LAKE

**ALEX PICKETT**

THE UNIVERSITY OF WISCONSIN PRESS

The University of Wisconsin Press
728 State Street, Suite 443
Madison, Wisconsin 53706
uwpress.wisc.edu

Printed in the United States of America
This book may be available in a digital edition.

Library of Congress Cataloging-in-Publication Data

Names: Pickett, Alex, author.
Title: Camera lake / Alex Pickett.
Description: Madison, Wisconsin : The University of Wisconsin Press, 2024.
Identifiers: LCCN 2023051401 | ISBN 9780299349141 (paperback)
Subjects: LCGFT: Short stories. | Fiction.
Classification: LCC PS3616.I284 C36 2024 | DDC 813/.6—dc23/eng/20231127
LC record available at https://lccn.loc.gov/2023051401

*For*
Elena

# Contents

# CAMERA LAKE

# Practice

I instituted a rule. Since they weren't mature enough to both play freshman football and police themselves, they were to put their phones in a big canvas bag before practice. They groaned. But they groan about everything.

On maybe the third day I realized the rule had potential beyond simply eliminating distractions. There was this one boy on the offensive line who could not grasp the concept of snapping the ball "on two." Frustrating for so many reasons, but foremost because the nature of the penalty meant that no play could be run. Practice kept grinding to a halt. After about the thirtieth time, I snatched off my visor and was about to ream him out when our equipment manager—John, a nice farm boy a couple of years younger than the players—handed me the canvas cell phone bag.

I'm pretty sure John was only fulfilling his duties by bringing me the phone sack. I had asked him a few minutes before not to leave it unattended in the locker room. But those phones gave me an idea. I put my visor back on and cleared my throat.

"The next time anyone moves a muscle before that ball is snapped," I said, "I will reserve the right to take their phone out of this bag"— I held up the bag—"and text whoever I want whatever I want."

Everyone laughed except Terry Hagadorn, the boy who couldn't remember the snap count. The other kids shouted out which girl to text on Terry's behalf. They whispered among themselves things they would never allow me to hear. The stunt energized the squad.

The next play Terry was a rock. For about five seconds after the ball was snapped, the kid stayed in his stance and ended up getting knocked on his ass by the scout-team nose tackle. But hey, after the day we'd been having, I'd take it. Nobody made a mistake for the next four plays, which was maybe a record for us, until our tight end—tall kid with good hands named Eric Duoss—jumped early. I had John fish out his phone.

I called Eric over and asked him to unlock it. A smart kid, this Duoss. The type you get every so often who succeed because they understand the game. It was a little satisfying to catch him out first, make sure he knew he wasn't all *that* clever. He complied with a little grin, like he was curious to see where this was going.

I didn't have a next move. I certainly wasn't going to text a girl like the team wanted me to. Get the student body involved in this and you have no idea where it's going. There was a lot of hooting, so I milked the suspense while figuring out what to do. I hemmed and hawed as I scrolled his contacts until I saw "Dad."

I clicked it. The texts were logistical. Arrival times home and dinner consumption. Anyone else—Terry Hagadorn, for instance—and I probably would have grilled him and let him off the hook without sending anything. Or I would have written Jim Hagadorn something like, *Hi Dad, I jumped offside twenty times today and wasted everyone's time at practice. Especially Coach's, who has better things he could be doing. Apparently I don't know the difference between going on one and on two. Maybe some extra chores would help me learn.* Me and Jim could have had a laugh about it at his hardware store.

Eric Duoss didn't flinch when I glanced up at him. I imagined he was doubting my ability to creatively follow through. I didn't know anything about his father. Since Eric wore glasses and was in the honors program, I pictured his father working at a desk, calculating, making a lot of money. I imagined he was a microbiologist or college professor. We held eye contact. Eric's smile grew.

"Got it," I said.

I typed, *Dad, I love you.* I hit send.

I handed him the phone. His smile disappeared and he paled.

"What the hell!" he yelled. "Coach, you can't do that!"

I'll be honest, I did question myself. But I couldn't back down. You can't show weakness on the practice field.

"Listen to the call next time," I said, as though this was a normal teachable moment.

He stared at me with his mouth open for so long that the tittering of the rest of the team died down. An uncomfortable silence fell upon the field. Duoss handed John the phone.

Back in the huddle, Duoss must have told the rest of the players what I did, because they all raised their heads and looked at me in horror. I clapped my hands and said, "Let's go! Clock's ticking!"

They got their asses in gear after that. All the rest of practice we only had three more false starts—easily the fewest we've ever had. I texted those boys' fathers as well.

That night, sitting on my porch grading take-home tests and drinking some Keystone Light, worry crept upon me. First I considered it practically, like maybe one of the kids' fathers was dead. I would have heard about that though. It's a small school. Even within normal father-son dynamics something about it felt itchy and vaguely obscene. It's not like I sent one of their mothers a picture of my johnson. Though maybe given the choice they'd prefer that. Couldn't put my finger on why. Maybe because I had never told and never planned on telling the same thing to my own father? Maybe because I'd rather someone text a picture of my johnson to my mother? Maybe because if I had a son and he texted that to me I wouldn't know what to do since I had never been taught to process such an excess of emotion?

My dog scrambled back to the porch barking her head off. She'd been out there in the woods horsing around, and emerged from the pitch black, covered in mud and twigs and leaves, running ninety miles per hour like she stole something. She scratched at the door and did a little let-me-in dance, but I was curious about why. She knew the deal with me, that I wouldn't open the door at all if I didn't right away, so she gave up dancing and crouched behind my chair, knocking the table and spilling my beer.

"What is it, girl?" I asked, laughing a little.

She whined, ears straight back.

I turned away from her, scared myself now, but nothing else emerged.

"You're just a scaredy-cat, aren't you," I said.

She whined.

"Just a widdle scaredy-cat," I said.

The next day the team was dressed and on the field before John handed me my whistle. This was highly unusual for my ragtag squad.

To kill their mood a little I said loudly to John, "Got the phones?"

John grinned and shook the phone bag like he was riling up a bunch of hornets.

Until I saw them doing their best to please me, I wasn't convinced I should double down. Whether I kept on because the method was effective or because not continuing would be tantamount to admitting fault, I am still unsure.

I expanded the punishment to include other offenses. I'd text the father of the player who came in last during sprints and of anyone who swore. I texted two more fathers before the first water break. During that break, while John and I were setting up cones for a round of hamburger, Eric Duoss approached with the grim look of an emissary from a country that was feeling recently aggrieved by its more powerful neighbor.

"Coach," Eric said, looking me in the eye, "I don't think the texting punishment is fair."

"That so?" I said, taking a cone from John.

"It was super awkward at home last night. My dad asked me if everything was all right. He thought I was in a car crash, that I was on life support and only had enough time left to send one text. Then he smelled my breath to make sure I wasn't drunk."

"What did you tell him?" I asked, curious about how such an interaction would go down and buying myself some time.

"I told him the truth, that I jumped before the snap and instead of having me run laps or something you texted my dad that I loved him for some reason."

"What did he say?" I asked.

"I don't know. He might have been a little hurt that it hadn't been for real. He got all quiet and spent the rest of the night in his study. It was really awkward, Coach."

"All the more reason to keep the snap count in mind, I guess," I said.

He sighed, obviously dismayed. "Can we at least just keep it to false starts and offsides, stuff we can control?"

You know you have them once they start trying to cut a deal.

"Seemed like everyone had an extra bounce in their step during conditioning today," I said. "You guys ran harder than you ever had before."

"I mean, you know that Stewart has asthma so he can't help coming in last during sprints. I don't think it's right that he was punished."

That was true about Stewart. He had a point there.

"Make sure you're hydrated before we start back up again," I said.

After a round of hamburger and then Oklahoma drills, we separated the starters from the scout team to run through some plays.

The tension was palpable. Before each snap they nodded at each other gravely, like soldiers before battle. They held firm. For a while I thought this was how it must feel to coach the New England Patriots. Just as I was figuring how I could parlay my new method to coach the varsity, or maybe score a smalltime college job where I wouldn't also have to teach, or even how I could turn this into a book and live off speaker's fees at coaching clinics, Eric Duoss, of all people, jumped early.

I shrieked my whistle and called him over. John fished his phone from the sack. Duoss stood still, hanging his head, his hands gripping his face mask in frustration. I blew my whistle again.

"Ah, come on, Coach," he whispered when he finally made his way over. His voice was shaky.

John thrust the phone at him and held it at arm's length.

"I won't do it," Eric said. "I'll quit. This isn't fair."

"Go on now," I said with genuine sympathy, surprising myself. "Go on and unlock it. You jumped."

"I know, but it isn't worth this. It's just practice. It's only freshman football."

"Go on now!" John shouted, shaking the phone. I touched my equipment manager's head to calm him.

Duoss turned toward the rest of the team.

"This is crazy, right?" he yelled. "He can't do this. We can just walk out. He needs us more than we need him. Without us there isn't a team."

"You're only digging yourself deeper," I said calmly, knowing nobody would join in his revolt. "Just go on and unlock it. It'll be over before you know it."

He glared for a moment at his cowardly teammates before he allowed his shoulders to slump. He took the phone from John.

This time I knew what I was going to write:

"Hey Dad. Remember when I told you yesterday that Coach sent you that text? Well, I lied. It was me. I was too embarrassed to admit it in person. It's easier to text about these kinds of feelings and stuff, I guess. Anyway, just know that I do love you but that if you ask me in person about this text I'll deny writing it and give some weird excuse like that Coach did it to punish me, like that makes any sense. Coach is a good guy though. I shouldn't have blamed him.

After I sent it I reached his phone toward him. He waved it away and slunk back to the huddle.

That night I was back on my porch with my Keystone, kind of wishing I had some papers to grade. A hot night. My dog had not yet come in from the woods though it was past her dinner. Sitting so alone I couldn't help but wonder what was going on at the Duoss's house right then. If maybe Eric and his father were playing a game of cribbage or chess before heading off to bed. Or perhaps he was helping Eric with his advanced-level homework, a hand resting on his gifted son's shoulder.

I grabbed another beer out of the minifridge I keep on my porch. I stood and peered into the darkness, listening for rustling or barking or whining. By the end of practice almost every player's father had been texted once, and three had been texted for a second time. Oddly, one of the only boys to escape punishment was Terry Hagadorn, the boy whose ineptitude kicked things off. At some point I must have gone too far. The juice that had flowed soon turned into frayed nerves. The players began snapping at each other and getting into fistfights on the sidelines.

"Dolly!" I yelled into the darkness. "Dinner!"

Perhaps I could call my own father. Not, of course, to profess my love, or to get advice, but just to see how he's holding up. I had spoken to my mother the previous Sunday, as usual, and she yelled to him, as usual, that I was on the line. His voice carried from the living room: "Tell him the Packers need a safety who can tackle." My mother chuckled and said, "Got that?" And I laughed and said yes, I got that.

"Dolly!" I said again, louder this time. I stepped down from my porch to the edge of the illuminated portion of the lawn. "Dolly, for chrissake, it's time for your supper!"

I listened.

The next day the players were sitting on their helmets when I arrived on the field. I held out my hand for my whistle but John was nowhere to be seen.

"Where's John?" I asked the team as a whole.

They all turned their heads toward Eric Duoss. He stood and spoke as though from a prepared statement.

"When John came to collect the phones, we refused. Then he started reefing on Stewart with this yardstick he found in the coach's office, so

we had no choice but to put the bag over his head. To our surprise it
fit over his entire body, so we kept yanking until we were able to tie it.
We took things a little too far and dragged him into the shower, telling
ourselves it was to cool him off. But really we were just tired of him. We
know it was wrong."

"Is he still in the shower now?" I asked, trying to keep cool but feeling my voice waver.

Eric answered, "He's in the shower room, tied in the sack, but the
shower itself is not on. He was still thrashing around, so we didn't want
to move him anymore. While we were dragging him he kicked Kurt so
hard he broke his pinkie."

Behind him Kurt held up his hand, displaying a gruesomely dislocated
finger.

"Kurt," I said, "go to the nurse before she leaves for the day." I doubted
Kurt's family had good insurance and wanted him to take advantage of
whatever free health care could be provided, even if only a rudimentary
splint and medical tape.

"Westrick and Ostertag," I said to our two middle linebackers, "go to
the locker room and untie the bag. Make sure to apologize to John before
you free him, though he probably deserved what he got. He thought he
was only doing his job."

They got up and jogged toward the school.

"I know this week has been rough," I said. "Though we have had
fewer false starts and offside penalties than we've ever had before, it's
difficult when those improvements come with a change in personal
relationships."

I had written and memorized this speech during sixth period while
my students took a pop quiz. The players shifted around, trying to get
comfortable as I spoke.

"But this was a *desired effect*," I continued. "I have never told my own
father I love him. He has never said the words to me. I thought this tactic
would not only cut down on penalties but improve your lives. It's best
if things like this are taken care of early, when you are still young."

"Then why don't you do it?" Eric chimed in. "If you wanted us to have the experience then why don't you text your father? You're still rather young and your father is apparently still alive."

"Three laps," I said.

A vexed look came over his face. He took off running.

As Duoss rounded the bend, the three boys returned from the locker room. John was sopping wet and chasing the other two with a yardstick. And though, stick or no stick, those linebackers could have beaten him to a pulp, they allowed John his moment.

I called to John and he immediately diverted his path toward me, not unlike how Dolly gives up chase on a squirrel when I say her name. The comparison brought a lump to my throat. She never returned home last night.

John sat beside me and bowed his dripping head in shame. "They wouldn't give them over," he said breathlessly. "I tried to make them but they shoved me in the sack."

I nodded kindly by way of apology. I couldn't verbally admit wrong-doing. In the unlikely case that charges were brought against me I wanted my union rep to have a fighting chance.

"The lesson here is about sports and life." I was finally able, after all the interruptions, to continue my planned speech. "Normally the only times you send texts like those are when you are on the verge of death or extremely drunk. That you were able to send them without suffering any physical harm or extreme regret or introspection is akin to how in sports you are able to feel the extremes of emotion and inflict and endure pain within the confines of a sanctioned activity. Though it appears now that perhaps I went too far, I see no reason why you should go through all this practicing if there aren't any real-world implications."

Most of the boys were watching the cross-country runners practice.

"One day," I continued, going off script, "when your father is on his deathbed, you will be thankful that I sent these texts. Also, in the short term, your fathers will be proud that you aren't committing stupid mental errors on the field. I'm telling you now that, no matter what they tell you, they are embarrassed when you do."

I needed to wrap it up. Not only was Eric almost finished with his laps but I was losing my train of thought. I was, after all, pretty exhausted after spending most of the night in the woods fruitlessly searching for Dolly.

"Now, does anyone have anything to share about the texts?" I asked. "About how your father reacted or, if he did not react, how that lack of a response made you feel?"

They all, to a man, were staring at the cross-country athletes now, though it is the most boring sport to watch. For the first time I wished Eric was around. At least he could articulate his thoughts.

"What I was wondering," came a voice so near to me that I almost jumped, "was why you didn't text my father anything." It was John. He was looking up at me with those forlorn eyes of his. My heart broke. "Is it because I don't have a phone?"

Before I could answer that, as far as I could tell, John had been left out because he had made no mistake, another boy, my slot wide receiver, said, "Consider yourself lucky he didn't. My dad was so happy last night he made me go fishing. I got a poison ivy rash all over my hands now."

In order to not discourage future contributions, I resisted pointing out that, as someone who often caught the ball, it might be best if he wore gloves from now on.

"At least he said something about it," my kicker said. "My dad wouldn't even look at me last night. My mom had to work late and we heated up some lasagna and didn't say a word the entire meal."

"You should get him to text him again," said the quarterback, one of the boys whose father I texted twice. "It was uncomfortable the first night, but whatever coach wrote yesterday really calmed my old man down. He still didn't say anything, or make much eye contact, but he gave me two hundred bucks for no real reason."

Eric finished his laps and stood there huffing at the edge of the group.

"What are you guys talking about?" he asked between gasps.

"Two more laps," I said. We were doing fine without him.

The boys all chimed in about their experiences. Our left guard, who everyone calls Tommy Pumpkin, said last night his father got really drunk sitting at the kitchen table and later that night stood unsteadily over Tommy for twenty minutes while Tommy pretended to sleep. And then he just walked out of the room. Our safety said his father told him a story about his time in Iraq, about how he shot and killed a civilian once because he wouldn't stop his car driving through a checkpoint. Apparently it was the first time his father had ever mentioned the war in front of his kid. Stewart, the unathletic boy with asthma who didn't exactly have a designated position, said that his father hugged him for several minutes as soon as he walked through the door after practice. Stewart explained that his father's father died last year and that the text and subsequent hug perhaps provided a release for him. Stewart still appeared unnerved by the interaction, though I know that one day he will be glad to have had it.

Eric had long before rejoined us but was too tired to add his two cents. I hoped hearing the others' stories put the experience into perspective for him. And perhaps it did since he stopped raising objections and spearheading mutinies. I considered forcing him to admit I had been right all along but worried he would point out that this was not my intended outcome when I first texted his father. That back then I only wanted to punish Eric for being smart and curious and for having a brighter future than I ever had.

We began to lose momentum, so I clapped my hands and said, "Let's go! Clock's ticking! Starting offense and scout team D on the field. We'll skip conditioning tonight."

They let out a rousing cheer at not having to run sprints. Everyone got into position. The first play, Terry Hagadorn jumped before the ball was snapped and I whipped off my visor in frustration, but I did not tell John to fish out his phone. I was just about to lay into Terry when I heard, off in the distance, a dog bark.

# At the Twin Pines Motel

She'd been staying at the Twin Pines Motel for two nights when she found the motel manager leaning back in a swivel chair in the rear office, like he was catching a nap. When she realized he was dead, she wasn't as shocked as she could have been. She just slipped the thirty dollars cash back into her pocket. She attributed her cool reaction to the high school years she spent working in a nursing home, where she came upon old dead folks like this from time to time. A guy she'd worked with used to call them *ploppers* because it looked like they'd just plopped down and died. She'd never liked when he said this—she thought it was a cold thing to say—but now as she gazed at the motel manager, the word kept going through her head. *Plopper.*

She studied the man and remembered the empty feeling the sight of a lifeless body used to give her. It seemed like a long time since she'd felt this. She took a deep breath and wiped her palms on her jeans. There was nothing to be done—he had been dead for a while. An old man who probably died of a heart attack or stroke while going through his mail. On the floor was a torn envelope. Junk mail from AARP. This seemed to her like a better way to go out than in an easy chair in a nursing home, but still not a particularly desirable end. She was at an age and a time in her life where the moment of death held the possibility of excitement or fascination.

She patted the thirty dollars in her pocket and went out to the tidy little lobby to take the master key, so she could get into all the rooms. A friend of hers back in Maine was the night auditor at a similarly wood-paneled, single-storied inn along the highway where people came if their car broke down or they couldn't afford a name-brand hotel or they desired anonymity. Back when she visited her friend at work, they used the master key to get into customers' rooms and root through their things while they were out. Neither she nor her friend took anything—except once when her friend took a sample-sized bottle of perfume because there was no way something that small would be missed—but the glimpses into other people's lives had been thrilling, more interesting even than the danger that came with breaking into the rooms. Once they had found a loaded handgun in an old lady's travel bag and another time discovered that a man had two large suitcases that were completely empty, as though he had just lost everything. Now, after discovering the manager's body, she decided to steal the master key, but did not intend to steal anything. Her thinking was that if she hesitated those doors would never be open to her.

The keys hung on hooks behind the desk. She counted them, twenty-nine, found the one with an *M* engraved on it instead of a number, walked outside, and opened the first room to the right to make sure the key worked. Then she went back inside, where the old man sat as though lost in thought, and called the police. Before exiting the office to go outside and wait for the police, she stopped in the doorway and said out loud, "Poor guy, all alone like that."

The motel was off the highway about ten miles from a town named Sparta. She had left home four days before, and this was the second motel she had stayed in since. Though she had enough money—for now—to stay in a Super 8 or Motel 6, she sought out places like the Twin Pines. These highway motels held a certain romantic appeal to her ever since she was a little girl. Her mother used to watch old movies where people stayed in similarly lousy places. Not just *Psycho*, but also scratchy old noirs where people at the ends of their ropes stumbled in through the rain and, desperate to get dry, asked the wary motel manager if there were any rooms available. For months she had felt a similar desperation and so these motels fit her state of mind, made her feel pursued though nobody was after her.

Two state policemen came and asked her questions. She said she had never seen anyone else working at the front desk other than the old man, and she didn't know anything beyond that. She also told them she was staying there because she had walked out on her husband. They didn't need to know this, but she felt relief after she said it. That was the first time she had said it out loud. The younger of the two troopers nodded at the ground, but the other looked her in the eye, as though to gauge if she was lying. She didn't tell him that she had also abandoned her five-month-old daughter.

They said she needed to leave the motel, and she argued, lying that she had paid through the end of the month and at least was entitled to a refund. She lied automatically, figuring they wouldn't look it up. They said she could take it up with whoever took over the place next and she relented, proud that she got away with her lie even though it didn't get her anything.

"Plenty of hotels around here," the older policeman said when she asked where she was supposed to stay. They stared at her until she went back to her room and gathered her things. Before she left, they made her give them the key to her room, and as she handed it over the older one looked at her suspiciously. She had never been looked at like that before, his eyes placid but heavy like he knew what she was up to and didn't care. What she had done to deserve that look she didn't know.

That evening she drove back to the motel and parked way in the back of the lot, where her car couldn't be seen from the highway. The other cars and trucks that had been there that morning were all gone. She let herself into her old room. For a moment she didn't turn on the light and could hear her heart beating in her chest. The brink-of-insanity anxiousness she had felt since her daughter was born returned, and she expected the phone to ring, to shatter the silence and make her jump, but nothing happened other than some jangling in the pipes. Her name was Anne, but she had told the police it was Abby. She lied so they would have a harder time figuring out who she was, should they come looking for her. Now that lie was all she could think about, as though it had been worse than stealing this motel room. Stealing, perhaps, wasn't the right word—you can't steal a room. But there was something wrong about what she was doing. She knew that.

She had left home without a plan. Now she was killing time while figuring out what to do. For almost five months, ever since giving birth to her daughter, she had been overcome by a trembling unease. She had wanted so badly to be a mother, but after she returned home from the hospital and things calmed down, she didn't feel anything when she held her daughter except the certainty that she had made an irrevocable mistake. Something was wrong with her, she knew, so she refused to tell anyone how she felt and pretended everything was normal. After four months, and despite his protests, she told her husband—who was twenty-nine and already a journeyman electrician who made plenty of money—that she was starting back working at the old folks' home, even though she had been fired and couldn't go back if she wanted to. After that, five days a week she would drop off the baby at his mother's and drive around the hills outside of their home in Bangor, Maine.

Ultimately, this scheme caused her even more stress since she was always worried about getting caught. But it was worth it for the moments of complete freedom where she did nothing but guide the car along winding roads and listen to Z104, the popular radio station she had listened to just a year and a half before, when she was in high school. Three weeks after she told her husband she had started working again and less than a week before she checked into the Twin Pines Motel, she had the attack that sent her to the hospital in an ambulance. She had been driving to her mother-in-law's house to pick up her daughter when she suddenly couldn't breathe. She pulled over, got out, fell, and convulsed on a bus stop bench, where someone called 911. She had been sure it was her heart and that she was about to die. After they convinced her that she wouldn't die, she only worried her husband would find out about the hospital visit and know she wasn't working. Once released, she took a cab to her car and drove west, only stopping at the bank to take out money.

Her plan was to get in touch with the guy she used to work with, the guy who called old dead people *ploppers*. Back when they worked together, when she was sixteen and in high school and he was thirty-two and divorced, they used to go into unoccupied rooms in the old folks' home and screw whenever they had the chance. This was before she had met her husband, and though she was already looking forward to being married, she never thought this guy would be the one. With him there had been none of the tenderness or devotion she expected from a man who loved her. Back then she just couldn't believe a guy twice her age would pay any serious attention to her, so she thought herself lucky to be able to have sex in empty rooms or in the back of his car during their lunch break. A few times, she even slept over at his place after telling her mom she was staying at the motel where her friend worked.

Eventually they were caught at work by the janitor and the guy moved to Seattle. But she didn't have any regrets, even though she was fired and her mom threatened to send her away to a Catholic high school, despite not being Catholic. She had considered this the most exciting time of her rather dull life, until now.

The guy had given her the phone number where he said he'd be staying in Seattle, but that was almost three years ago. Nobody picked up when she had called from the motel the first night after she left her child and husband. If she could get in contact with him, now that she was of legal age, she thought maybe they could be together, and she could recapture the feeling of wrongness and excess their sleeping together had once produced.

The Twin Pines Motel was about halfway across the country and far away from Bangor. She supposed she'd stay here another day or two to figure out if she wanted to keep going west to look for this guy or to return home. Now that she had the master key, she thought this was as good a place as any to stop for a while, since it was free.

She stayed in the room twenty-four hours straight without leaving, the TV always on and the blackout curtains drawn. She called the number of the guy in Seattle thirty-two times, but nobody ever picked up. Calling him turned out to be a comfort, almost a game. She'd call and place the receiver on the table by the window and turn down the TV really low and listen to the pulse of the ring coming from across the room. Sometimes she tricked herself into believing someone had picked up, and she would run over and push the receiver breathlessly to her ear. She didn't know what she'd say if he picked up. Twice she dialed all but one number of her home phone.

After the cops kicked her out of the motel, she had gone to town and bought enough groceries to last her for a few days. There was no refrigerator in the room, so she bought Pop-Tarts and Ritz Crackers and Coke and bread and peanut butter and cans of food like beans 'n' franks. She also bought a can opener and a *Penthouse* magazine. She grabbed the magazine on a whim, remembering how the posed, sweaty-looking bodies made her feel when she used to sneak into her brother's room and steal glances at such magazines he kept hidden under his mattress. The gas station attendant made her show ID to prove she was eighteen and then scrutinized it, and her, for a long time, before he grinned and handed her card back.

At first it had been fun hunkering in. It felt like camping or hiding out after committing a crime. But by the end of the second day, she was sick of eating junk and masturbating and calling the guy in Seattle and watching talk shows and sitcom reruns. She kept the TV on constantly so she wouldn't feel so alone. The TV was on even when she slept or masturbated or once when she stripped completely naked and cleared out enough space to perform every cheer she had learned during the half a season she was a B-squad cheerleader for the JV football team. Soon she started to feel sorry for herself, since this was all she could think to do for amusement.

The second night, after it got dark outside, she called the Seattle number one more time. When no one answered, she turned off the TV and left the room. She took her master key and started in the back and opened all the rooms one by one, looking for the best one. They were basically all the same—one exposed room taken up mostly by a low, queen-sized bed with a thin, scratchy comforter, tile floors, mismatching side tables and dressers probably bought secondhand. But some of the faucets didn't work right or the shower was moldy, or the TV remote didn't have batteries. Mostly they all smelled of cigarettes and dust and old sex. She was used to her room by now, so she kept it, but took anything she wanted out of the others. She took an additional mattress and a bunch of new pillows and less scratchy sheets and all the towels and sixteen extra bedspreads. She took the Bibles.

By midnight she had gone through all twenty-eight of the other rooms, then she went back to hers and surveyed the heap of linen. She had no idea why she had gone to the trouble but didn't regret it.

For a long time, she sat on the edge of her bed. Until she heard the crunch of tires on the parking lot gravel, a car door close.

For the next hour she did little but check to make sure the blackout curtains were pulled tight. She kept as quiet as possible. Every so often the sound of a closing door or the clattering of pipes filling with water pierced the silence.

She wouldn't be able to sleep knowing there was someone else at the motel. She wanted to call her husband, since his best feature may have been providing practical advice about this type of thing. But if she called, he'd only tell her to come home.

She let her mind run away with her. She considered writing her real name and home address down on a piece of paper and hiding it in a drawer in case this person broke in and killed her and stole her purse. Somehow the act would comfort her. She thought about this all very seriously and then laughed out loud for being so reasonable about the perverse thought of her own death.

Just as she laughed, there was a knock on the door and she blurted out, "Who is it?" then covered her mouth with her hand.

"Hello?"

She kept quiet. Another knock.

"Hey," said a tentative voice, "my name is Richard. No one else is here."

"Yes," she said.

"All right. Sorry to bother you, but I saw the light on. I just took a shower and there wasn't any towels," he said, and paused. When she didn't respond he added, "And I was wondering if you had any." Again, she said nothing. He said, "Because I'd like to dry off."

She glanced over at the huge pile of folded towels just outside the bathroom door. She wondered how she could get him one without opening the door, and ridiculously considered if there was some way to utilize the air ducts.

"And my bed doesn't have any blankets," the man said hopefully.

"Richard," she said, allowing desperation into her voice, "you're not going to kill me, are you?"

"Ma'am, I'm out here wet and wrapped in the fitted sheet from the bed. I just want a towel."

"You know I almost died once?" Anne asked him later, in his room. She had told him to go back there and wait and then had gathered up several towels and an extra set of sheets and blankets, folded them up, and brought them by. She was going to just knock and leave them outside the door, but she didn't like the idea of linens getting dirty. He had taken the sheets and thanked her with an odd expression on his face. When he began closing the door, she asked if she could come in for a bit. He hesitated and said she could. She was troubled by how he wanted to close the door. It felt as though she had done something to offend him. Plus, she hadn't talked to anyone since she'd gone to town two days before, when she got a Coke at a Denny's and talked to an old couple at a nearby table. Now she was anxious for company. She wanted to convince him that she was staying at the motel legitimately, so she started talking about her life as though they were simply fellow travelers.

"What's that?" he called from the bathroom, where he was finishing drying off.

"I almost died!"

"Okay," he said.

"I was seventeen and had kind of a heart attack. No real reason— no, there was, but I won't go into it—I didn't do anything to deserve it though. The doctors just told me that it happens sometimes with some people, like I was born with it. I take pills now. They said I died for about thirty seconds, but I've always thought of it as a long pause between heartbeats."

"Can you hand me that?" He had come in from the bathroom while she was yelling to him, and now indicated his duffel bag that was on the ground between her legs. He was wrapped in a small, thin towel, and she saw how embarrassed he was to have her there, probably because of how his shoulders folded in on his concave chest. His chest hair only grew in tufts around his nipples and on the side of his abdominals like a row of brambly bushes on either side of the gently sloping path of his swollen little pot belly. Between his chest and his right shoulder, just above the armpit, was a small green tattoo of a cheetah stretched out in full sprint. She had never seen a tattoo in this spot on anyone before and was going to comment on its strangeness but figured she had no business making him more self-conscious than he already was.

She handed him the duffel and he walked quickly back to the bathroom. When he was out of sight, she continued speaking.

"Why I had Birdie. That's my daughter." She swallowed down fear or sadness when she said her daughter's name. "I figured if I was going to die, I wanted to have a baby first, have a family, to know what that's like. It never crossed my mind to see the world or screw a bunch of boys. Went right to finding a husband. Probably how I was raised."

She waited for a response, but all she heard was a quiet grunt from the other room, like he was having a hard time getting his leg into his pants or just slipped a bit on the wet floor.

When he came back in, she said, "I still think I'm going to die, every day I think it could happen."

He looked alarmed and said, "I'm sorry?"

"It's no big deal. Anyone could die every day."

"No." He looked as though he wasn't sure if he should go on, then said, "I didn't hear what you've been saying. I wasn't paying attention."

She didn't feel like telling it all again and felt cheated at having just wasted her best story. It took energy to tell that story, and she was used to it getting a certain response. Even though he hadn't been listening, with the absence of a reaction she doubted how good of a story it really was. Maybe, she thought, from now on *this* would be her new best story. The story of her staying at this motel, being in this odd man's room. It seemed impossible she would ever tell this to anyone though, no matter what she did after she left.

He sat on the other side of the bed and fiddled with the TV remote, spinning it in the air and catching it. He was dressed in wrinkled corduroys and a dirty, buttoned-up denim shirt. Anne wondered if his dirty clothes were itchy now that he was clean.

"I saw an accident earlier today," he said suddenly, still flipping the TV remote.

"Was it bad?"

"On the interstate. I saw it coming too. Saw the car a few hours earlier and knew it was going to crash. It wasn't driving reckless or speeding too much. I just knew." He scrunched his nose and said, "I see things like that."

"How do you mean?"

"I can just see things that will occur. Not like ESP or whatever. I just see people or animals or clouds or whatever and know what's going to happen to them. Like how sometimes you can see a lamp and just know the light bulb in it will be burnt out."

Anne had no idea what he meant.

"I'm more attuned," he said as a kind of conclusion.

"I think I know what you mean," Anne said brightly to fill the ensuing silence. "Like now, I see my life going in one direction or another. I can either go west or east, you know? And I can see how each of them will play out in full. I see how my birthday five years from now will either be me making us all a cake or else being in a place where nobody even knows it's my day, or how one day I'll see my daughter graduate high school or else the next time I'll see her is when she'll track me down years from now when she needs a kidney or something." Saying this out loud hit Anne like a fist, and she put a hand to her mouth. She didn't even know those thoughts had existed within her.

Richard only shook his head hard. "That's not it at all," he said. "Those are just choices you make. Should-I-pullover-at-this-stand-and-buy-this-Indian-jewelry stuff. What I mean is really knowing. Like a couple weeks ago"—he glanced at her to make sure she was following him—"I saw this kid walking across the street and thought how he'll be in prison. Next week, I saw his mug shot in the paper. That was in Sarasota, Florida."

"Maybe it was a different person? In the paper. Maybe he just looked like him."

"It was him all right," he said with a laugh, as though she was stupid.

"I'm more interested in what I'm going to do than if some kid's in prison or not," she said.

"I don't doubt that," he said, more animated than she'd seen him. "Me, I like to look how things will play out. Like I'll be watching a baseball game and know just before a pitch if it'll be a home run or not. Then to see it happen!"

She didn't press him. She didn't believe for one second that he had any insight, and she didn't want to hear any other crazy ramblings. But she liked being near someone else, even if he was strange. And having seen him in that towel took away any lingering fear she may have had of him. Anything that pathetic couldn't possibly harm anyone.

He turned on the TV. There was a news program on PBS. Anne wished anything else was on the screen—anything would be better. But she didn't ask him to change the channel. It wasn't her room. Instead, she asked him why he was at the motel, if he was traveling somewhere.

"Me?" he said, not taking his eyes away from the screen. "I own this motel."

"But he died," Anne said, then bit hard on her tongue with her eyetooth.

"I'm his nephew," he said, eyes still on the TV. "Guess I don't own it yet. Have to sign some papers, fill some things out, show two forms of government-issued ID, that kind of thing. Took care of things when the old man was on vacation, so I already had the keys. Been driving for two days ever since they called."

She didn't know what to say and instead paid attention to the TV, where there was a roundtable discussion involving three old men and a young woman.

"Don't you want to know who I am?" she asked after a minute.

"Figured you were taking care of things until my arrival," he said.

She stayed quiet.

"*Do* you work here?" he asked.

"No," she said. "I just needed a place to stay."

"Well, there you go," he said.

She didn't say anything, and he turned to her. He said, "Aren't you going to ask me for permission to stay?"

A feeling came over her, like she was walking along without a care and then stepped in a puddle of muddy, oil-slicked water. She had just been in an okay mood and now that mood was ruined. She got up from the bed and walked out.

On her bed, staring at the ceiling where the light from the muted TV flickered, she couldn't bring herself to move. All she wanted to do was call Seattle, but now she felt sure the guy would pick up, and that frightened her.

Outside she heard footsteps and then a tap on her door.

"Lady, you don't have to go," he said through the door. "Tell the truth, I was getting excited on the drive up here, thinking I'd sell this place, take the money, and move on up to Alaska. Now I'm not sure. I mean, it probably won't sell for much, taxes and all. But hell. Found money."

He paused for a long time.

"But now," he almost shouted, "I'm thinking I like it out here. Quiet. I don't have much going on. Can always fix it up, sell it later. If I did keep it, you could stay. Hell, you can live here permanent. Can help me run it if you want. I can live over there, and you live here. Pay you a wage."

She turned over and put one of her twelve pillows over her head and held it tight. He kept speaking but it was muffled. When she took the pillow off it was quiet, but she knew he was still out there.

"Richard?" she called.

"Right here."

"What do you see for me? What's going to happen?"

"How do you mean?"

"You see things. You said before you know what people are going to do. Tell me."

"I was kidding about all that," he mumbled so quietly that she crept off the bed and crawled to the door so she wouldn't miss anything. "I was trying to fool you. Just something to say. Sure, I see things but not really. I spend too much time alone."

"Richard," she said calmly through the door. "Tell me, Richard. I don't care if it's true, just tell me. Tell me what I'm going to do."

When he didn't speak, she went back to bed. To try to settle her mind, she imagined what was going on back at her house. Her mother-in-law there, sleeping in the baby's room. Her husband in bed unable to sleep. Her daughter crying, or needing to be changed, or staring at her mobile, or asleep in her crib. The idea of all that exhausted and depressed her.

In the morning, she knew, she would see things differently one way or another. But now, on top of two mattresses, surrounded with pillows, like a shabby queen, she didn't regret a single thing she had ever done. And no matter what happened next at least it would be her choice.

Outside, Richard began to speak. She was comforted by this strange man's presence. She liked that this was who she was right now, that this is who she'd become. She had no idea that she had been searching for this feeling until she found it.

From outside she heard a seemingly unending string of words come from Richard, all muffled and indecipherable. She thought how tomorrow would be different, but right here and now she was in the perfect place. She was tired but tried to keep from sleeping, because when she woke up it would be tomorrow. At this moment she was right where she was supposed to be. She wanted to be who she was right now forever.

# PETLAND

1

Every day there's new, weird trash in this overgrown field between my apartment complex and the interstate. A rusty wheelchair, baby clothes, cracked IKEA juice cups, an old iPod, mattresses—there one day and gone the next. Admiring the trash was a pleasant distraction as I walked through the long grass that made my ankles itch the rest of the day. Better than staring at the stark white concrete of the interstate, waiting for a break in traffic, my blue Petland shirt already sweated through on hot days, my name tag whipping around. I'd run, hesitate, jump back and forth like a cat. Once across I'd spend the rest of the walk—down the embankment, across that forever parking lot—fixated on those interstate drivers, who were surely laughing at me, joking with coworkers about how they once again saw that crazy woman darting across all those lanes.

At least once I got to work there were dogs. Flopping around. No matter how down I was, seeing a bunch of romping puppies always briefly lifted my spirits. Like a cocaine bump. Then I'd see those locked cages with metal grates for floors so their mess could filter through. The sores on their feet made them step so daintily to get to their sad empty water dish. Balls of poop stuck in their fur. I'd hose down the stench first thing. The worst part was rinsing these four-inch-long hard rubber mats that we put in there for them to sleep on. We were told it's too difficult to clean soft things. The way they snuggled up against these rubber mats, like they were made of memory foam, broke my heart every time.

I only realized they were all puppy mill dogs when I googled the store after I was hired and saw a petition to close it down. These dogs, sired by tortured slaves, bred to be the cutest goddamn things you've ever seen. But wild! They just fight and shit and fight in their own shit, which never passes completely through the metal grating. Gawk for two minutes and you're smitten, but after the initial shock wears off, once the spell is broken, it's like being forced to take care of other people's children. I wanted to shake and slap them, but the effort of my care also made me protective. I'd often spend my breaks cuddling them, feeling their desperate little licks and bites and kicks as they tried to prove their love. My teeth began to ache from grinding.

I should have quit as soon as I saw those rubber mats. Definitely after I discovered they were from mills. Except I couldn't. For financial reasons, yes, but I also came to crave the company of beings worse off than me, someone I could actually care for. And those mats and the forced confinement made sense. I felt sentenced to work there. If my apartment's floor was switched to metal grating I could imagine being perfectly content sitting on a hard rubber island. Seeing these mistreated pups every day felt like exactly what I deserved.

2

There was this one dog. She came in maybe six months after I started. Some kind of bulldog mix. Heavy bags weighed down her eyes, showing all the pink viscera under her skin. Her fur knotted up a day after brushing. Her stump of a tail wagged high and proud. Plus she had a terrible sense of showmanship. She kept her openmouthed, tongue-exposed face away from the display window, which gave all the customers a perfect view of her butthole.

We weren't allowed to name them, so of course we always did. Dog names are always stupid—either too cute or too clever with the Mr. or

Mrs. So-and-sos, or they are ironically classic like Fido, or too human like Steve, or purposefully inappropriate like naming a fat ugly dog Petunia. We called this one, the showman, Mark McGwire. Someone else named her. I'm pretty sure it was a sports thing. At least we didn't stick to gender conventions.

Mark McGwire had no chance. When she first arrived, she was actually pretty cute. Her eyes, the tail, and the open mouth were charming when she was tiny, like a baby in a business suit. When they initially enter the store, we take their picture for the website, and Mark McGwire's didn't stand out. Perhaps she wasn't as symmetrical and regal as a sheltie pup, but she had the messy adorableness of a Jim Henson puppet. The minute she filled out though. Oh boy. Her price got reduced quicker than any dog since I'd gotten there. Less than a month in she went from $2,817 to $1,983—these precise, nonrounded numbers as though there's some exact *value*. And then down to sixteen hundred. Down to twelve. Like a painting that won't sell. Like a stock in free fall. It didn't help that this dog was female. I'll bet if Mark McGwire were male, he would have been snatched up and thought of as hilariously cute, but as a girl dog—yes, a bitch—she was hideous.

What's also fascinating is that because their price is reduced—*because of it*—people don't want them. They are seen as deficient. Reduced, deficient. And when, based on a corporate algorithm, we know nobody is going to take a dog, when the cost of upkeep outweighs the potential for profit and the dog becomes a financial burden, some winner from corporate comes, wearing a uniform, coveralls like a goddamn mechanic, and takes them. Where? I asked Penny, my boss, the first time one of these guys came. She shrugged and said, Back to the farm? Hard, hard Penny. I'd worked with Pennies before—hell, I might have *been* a bit of a Penny back when I still had a recognizable life, back when I laughed at people who lived in apartments that overlooked the interstate. So many Pennies in this world. Pennies were the lifers. They got the damn job done. Now I wept out back by the dumpsters during my break after the first time I saw a dog taken away. The tears wetting my cigarette filter. Exhaling with shaky breaths. Then going right back in to finish my shift.

I decided not to let the corporate mechanics take Mark McGwire away. She was the first dog I was certain wouldn't get adopted, and I couldn't sit back and watch it happen. There was nothing else I could do. So I kept an eye on her price, hoping it would get below a thousand, which would at least change her theft from grand to petty larceny. One day, though, when you don't expect it, that price won't be reduced any further. The mechanics give no warning.

3

I squirm to think of the tactics, though some of them ended up coming in handy for my Mark McGwire scheme. Basically it was implied during training that we were supposed to identify dumb people. To be on the lookout for customers who look bad with money and lazy— because why else wouldn't they go rescue a dog? —and ask if they want to take a pup to the Cuddle Zone, which is a wooden cubicle with a bench. After exactly two minutes we are to bring over an information sheet and casually mention our financing plans. Ten percent down, no interest for six months. If the customer asks about puppy mills, which is rare, we're to furrow our brow and check the information sheet and show them how the dog comes from "a farm in Iowa." A licensed breeder, not a mill. Of course it's from a mill! I always shout in my mind, as I tell them otherwise, because I need and want my job. We were also instructed to badmouth rescue shelters. If asked, we are required to say that shelters are "the real reason for pet overpopulation." We were also encouraged, but not required, to call the dogs "furry babies," though I never have, because I'd rather vomit.

And yet I still can't bring myself to blame the customers. Despite hating them for being stupid and lazy and buying these dogs, I can't hold them entirely responsible, because I can see they are powerless against those big puppy paws slapping against them and the sandpaper tongue against their cheek. Indeed, anytime I doubted my desire to save Mark

McGwire, all I had to do was give her a nuzzle to set myself straight. These idiotic prospective buyers really do just want something to love. They don't concern themselves with the fact that each dog they buy induces the mill to breed three more, two of which will probably die unnaturally or be used strictly for breeding. They also don't consider contingencies that could force them to default on a payment to a pet store and have to give up their dog.

There was one couple. One good, non-defaulting couple, who brought their corgi puppy back to the shop with them. I had apparently sold them their dog maybe four months before, when I first started working there. Four months is so long in this context—for me and the dog. I didn't recognize the dog or the couple. The dog because it was now the size of a hatchback and the couple because they were just some white dog-buying people. Plus I had sold so many dogs by then. One, two, three, up to six thousand a pop. So many. This couple told me that they took their corgi to a dog trainer and were informed that it wasn't a corgi at all. It was a mastiff. Well shit, I said. It was all I *could* say. I didn't know. I probably knew by then, actually, since I had started identifying breeds better. But even so the paperwork had said corgi. This thing could have eaten a corgi. When Penny walked by I made a desperate motion that got her attention. I pointed at the man, who had been doing all the talking. He exhaled and explained. Penny—hard, hard Penny— then, without so much as a sigh, said, We'll take him back if you want. I and the couple both recoiled like she shot a gun in the air. The man said, Well, no, we're attached. *Attached.* Like a wart. Then what would you like *us* to do? Penny asked, including me in the *us*. The man sputtered and we waited.

When they left I asked Penny what would have happened if they'd returned the dog. She told me it would have stayed in the back of the store for two months, and if the couple didn't reclaim it, it would "go back to corporate." This information would later prove vital for my plans with Mark McGwire. I then asked her why we wouldn't resell it, and in her distant, Penny way, she explained how the policy came about that we couldn't sell a dog twice. Apparently, a long time ago at some other branch of our store, they had resold a dog after someone defaulted on it and it happened to have been bought the second time by the original owner's neighbor. The original owners were then forced to watch this once cherished creature paraded around the neighborhood three times a day and its barking kept them up at night. Finally the neighbor stole it back and kept the dog locked in the basement for a month, before the dog's legal owner caught on and called the police. The subsequent lawsuits resulted in our current policy. It's almost like you shouldn't sell sentient beings to the highest bidder, I wanted to reply but was far too afraid of Penny to actually say. Who knew that playing with emotional bonds for profit can mess with people? I also didn't say.

I had known before I asked that the answer to my question would disturb me. But I was still glad to know. Something about being a part of an evil operation made me crave the details. Knowing exactly what I was doing gave my complicity structure and depth. My awareness made me feel more in control. Maybe in the same way that years ago I picked and picked at the cuticle of my thumb until it bled and since then I have sustained the wound, so now I need to feel it all the time, the pain becoming a kind of habit, or a comfort. Maybe on some level I know that if the wound were to heal and callus over I might feel the need to make another, one that might not be so safe.

4

Only women worked on the floor of the pet store. I'm not sure why this was. The only men involved with our Petland branch were the mechanics who took the drain-on-society dogs away; a veterinarian who gave vaccinations and treated the dogs' kennel cough with—according to information I found online—powerful vitamins and stimulants that mask the symptoms until after they are adopted; and the owner, who did not often show his face.

When the idea to save Mark McGwire first began to percolate, there was only one fellow employee I didn't mind, this girl just out of high school named Kelly, who was hired a few months after I started. Overweight, enthusiastic, not very bright, and so easy to be around. She probably thought of me like a fun, inappropriate aunt. My cigarettes. Sunglasses covering hangovers. Making fun of Penny behind her back. But I wasn't entirely sold on letting Kelly in on my plan to save Mark McGwire until I saw her weep the first time she witnessed the mechanics take an unsellable dog. I found her sobbing uncontrollably at the table next to the Coke machine, where, if we felt like being depressed, we could eat our lunch. So I took her by the hand and led her back to the dumpsters, which is a more appropriate place to cry because you can really let go and nobody will see you. I led her back there feeling like a grandfather taking his grandson to his favorite secret fishing hole, sneaking glances at the kid to make sure he was appreciating the full weight of the moment. I doubt she appreciated it fully but boy did she cry. I offered her a cigarette and she shook her head. I told her, Trust me.

There's so much puppy shit in those dumpsters. Soiled pee pads. Rotting dog food. The newspapers from under the bird and rabbit cages. Dead lizards. Cigarette butts littered the ground. It was like the tears were milked out of you back there. It emptied you. After crying by the dumpsters my tear ducts ached from overuse.

I propped open the door with one of those rubber mats we put in the cages. Kelly lit her cigarette and immediately began hacking out smoke and tears and snot. She gasped, Why don't we just give them away to someone who can't afford to buy them anyway? I patted her shoulder and was going to tell her some hard truths about capitalism, but held off. She added, Why do they have to die? Well, sweetie, I said, trying on the endearment like I once tried on a maternity "Cozy Wrap" cardigan at Target, everything has to die. She looked at me angrily. I apologized.

In the awkward moments that followed, I happened to look down at the mat propping open the door. Something clicked and I realized how I could actually get away with stealing Mark McGwire. Until then I'd assumed that I'd wait too long, panic, shove her in my bag one night on my way out of the store, and then pray that my audacity would protect me.

But now I was inspired, and blurted it all out to Kelly right away so I wouldn't lose my nerve. I told her that Mark McGwire was obviously the next to go. She nodded sadly. I said that we had to save her. Kelly asked how. I explained that we needed to get someone to buy her and default on her payments so she was held in the back of the store, since there were no cameras back there. Kelly said nothing. Then, I went on, when I was on the closing shift I'd prop the door open and sneak over in the middle of the night and steal her. All I needed Kelly to do was find the person to buy and return the dog, since I had burned all my bridges.

Won't it hurt their credit? was all she asked in response, tears still pouring down her face. Whose? I asked. The person who defaults on the dog, she answered. Who are you, Alan Greenspan? I asked. Who? she answered. I made something up about how the store's financing system was inhouse, and they wouldn't report it to a credit agency if the dog was returned after only one missed payment. I didn't want to tell her I hadn't thought everything through, though what I said might well have been true. This easy blurring of financial truths was a product of my pre-Petland life, back when I approved loans on dubious property shares for people who couldn't afford them. It wasn't significantly less upright than selling overproduced animals to gift-starved husbands on Christmas Eve, but now, making my wage, I was at least in no danger of being bankrupt and charged with fraud. They couldn't again take away my house and my partner since I no longer had a life worth repossessing. But if nothing else, at least I could put my ability to lie to good use with Kelly.

All she said when she finished her cigarette was, Okay, I gotta get away from this. By this she meant the dumpster. But she didn't say no to my plan. Back inside the store she could barely look at the dogs for the rest of the day.

## 5

From then on the Mark McGwire scheme became my obsession. When I'd put my hands over my face upon waking up, hoping this was not actually my life and feeling nearly certain that I could not face another day, Mark McGwire would come to mind and I'd fling myself out of bed. During a shift I'd run over the plan a hundred times in my head, playing out each step in excruciating detail—not honing the particulars so I wouldn't get caught, but simply because the fantasy gave me pleasure. It reminded me of how I used to replay particularly good dates in my head the next day, back when I used to go out on dates.

I was aware that there were more "proper" channels to go through. I could contact PETA, let them know I was desperate enough to be of use to them. Or I could reach out to local animal advocates. A handful of polite protesters had gathered outside the store once. I could have tried to track them down.

These do-gooders could have funded the operation, found someone to buy and return Mark McGwire and locate a family to take her in after I stole her. But I couldn't bring myself to go that route. I alone needed to save her. I didn't want them to have Mark McGwire. I pictured her face on a website as a mascot for their cause. It didn't feel any different from how her picture was currently posted on the pet store's site. It would turn her into a symbol and define her worth, when she was Mark McGwire and nothing else to me. I needed to risk everything for her. I didn't want the safety net of a justified arrest. I didn't want praise.

I educated myself about the risks. If caught I would lose my job, probably become homeless, and face felony charges. I found a news story about a couple who once walked out of a pet store with a pug hidden under the man's shirt. In addition to grand larceny, they were charged with felony retail theft and dognapping. Up to four years in prison. And you better believe that my store would prosecute to the fullest extent. I was aware of all this and still decided to proceed. One look at Mark McGwire and I knew I had no choice.

## 6

About a week later Kelly said she found someone to buy and return the dog. I did not like what that did to my heart rate. Who is it? I asked her. She said a friend, a guy. I kept asking if he was sure he knew what we were doing. She said he didn't care about doing it as long as he didn't have to spend his own money and could return Mark McGwire to the store after one month, so he didn't get harassed by debt collectors. I nodded slowly. Apparently I was now worried about this guy's credit score.

The kid came in a few days later. God, this boy. He did everything but wear a trench coat and sunglasses. He had these weird sideburns. The future of his credit rating was bleak anyhow. He paid the down payment with money I'd given to Kelly to give to him (money I raised by stealing an expensive tank filter and selling it online). When we finished with the paperwork, I slipped him my apartment keys and wrote my address on a discarded receipt.

That night I smelled her as soon as I opened my front door. I was immediately smitten. I found her under my bed, sleeping in a puddle of pee, and scooped her up and hugged her without even cleaning her off first. It was the happiest I had been in a long time.

Me and Mark McGwire had a grand time together after that. She breathed and drooled all over me. She went to the bathroom wherever she desired. She made perfect sense to me. Some nights I'd lie on the floor with my head on Mark McGwire's little butt and I wouldn't need rum or TV or anything. How could this dog possibly love me? I'd ask. And I wouldn't care about the answer.

About a month later, right around when the boy's first payment was due, Kelly told me she found someone to take Mark McGwire. Take her? I said and audibly gulped. Kelly looked confused. I was thinking I might just keep her, I said, though we both knew that two of our co-workers lived in my apartment complex. Kelly didn't want to have to tell me I couldn't. More the sidekick type, this one. I said, It's not like they're going to break down my door and search my house—she won't be hunted like a fugitive. Kelly, whose practicality emerged at the most annoying times, replied, But won't someone see you when you walk her? She was right, of course. I'd been smuggling out pee pads and handfuls of loose dog food in my purse. I'd cleaned a lot of shit off my floor. My apartment smelled like the pet store. Mark McGwire had only been outside in the dead of night. Still I gave it one more shot. Pee pads? I said. Kelly looked at her shoe and said, It's a terrible life if you can't go outside.

7

I began to understand suicide pacts. How you'd rather the other be dead if you can't be together, how it's worth it to die as long as nobody else can have your beloved. Of course I didn't kill Mark McGwire or try to kill myself. I hadn't lost all perspective. I was simply sad and had nothing. I did make Kelly give me the person's address who was taking her though. I got an Uber to drive me, as though I could afford *that*. But the house looked appropriate. Clean. A fence. SUV in the driveway. The pain of knowing who would take her. Seeing someone else so much better equipped. The last thing I wanted to consider was if I would switch places with them. Take their house and their fence and big car and Mark McGwire. If I had it I'd piss it away. I had it once and I pissed it away.

8

Six weeks after he bought her, the boy picked little Mark McGwire up from my apartment. Our last night together I cried so hard I threw up. Technically the store didn't accept returns, but if we had no other choice or accidentally took one back, it meant the dog was slated for the mechanics, so we made sure I handled the transaction, and that Penny wasn't working when he made the return. Penny had a knack for scaring people performing legitimate business. This boy would have peed his pants. The kennel where we stored the returned dogs was in a space behind the depressing break room. Cannot and will not describe the feeling of seeing Mark McGwire inside that little death chamber. That limbo. Her face when I shut and locked the door.

A month went by. Mark McGwire stared out of the kennel. I discovered my soul had the capacity to die even more each day. When I fed her I'd take an extra minute and scratch her sticky jowls, but wouldn't allow myself to linger so I didn't arouse suspicion. During one trip back there I realized that the limbo kennel faced the designated photo area, where we take pictures of the newly arrived pups before their fur becomes dull from cheap food and all that time spent under neon lights. Before the life goes out of their eyes. The vet who comes once a month also fancies himself a photographer and collects payments for both services. All his pictures, which are posted to the store's website, have a soft-lit, hazy glow like a closeup in an old movie. The dogs end up looking like coiffed hostages, pleading to get rescued. The background for the photos is light pink and someone painted yellow stars to make it look like a sky at sunset. It's perhaps supposed to look like heaven. This was what Mark McGwire was forced to look at all day. It seemed intended to rub her nose in her failure to be profitable.

One night when I closed the store I covered the hole in the doorframe with a matchbook so the back door didn't latch. This is the same door that leads out to the dumpsters. I then snuck back in at two that morning. Mark McGwire was awake and staring out the door of her cage even at that late hour. Her tail thumped against the kennel wall when she heard my voice, which provided me with a painful stab of love beyond what I thought I was still capable of feeling. I scooped her out. So warm. Melted. Breath on my arm. I snuck back out with her and let the door click closed.

## 9

The next day, when I saw Mark McGwire's empty cage in the back room, it took me a few minutes to grasp that she was truly out of reach of the mechanics. For a second I thought I was having a panic attack, but then understood I was just happy.

It took almost a full day before anyone noticed she was missing. The police were notified. There is an ongoing investigation but nobody has yet been specifically targeted. Penny seems more stressed—another small victory. I swear she has eyeballed me more than usual ever since it happened, but maybe I am just hoping that she suspects me and can't prove it. I hope that I am making her crazy.

I'd like to say I played it cool for the good of Mark McGwire. But after only a couple days I began spending most of my time outside of work riding the lonely A-21 bus clear across town so I could walk around Mark McGwire's new neighborhood to try to catch a glimpse. For almost two weeks I didn't see any sign of her. I began to worry that Kelly lied to me, that she kept Mark McGwire for herself and was trying to sell her, or was biding her time before returning her for the reward.

Finally, one day, just after dusk, minutes before I had to run the twelve blocks to catch the last bus back home, a woman poked her blond permed head out the back door and looked carefully both ways, as though checking if the coast was clear. I hid behind a tree. She turned back inside and stooped down to pick something up. I ran away.

If she had turned around without Mark McGwire in her arms, I wouldn't have been able to take it. I also couldn't see Mark McGwire again, not from that far away. But not knowing gave me a reason to come back, even if I have not since made the trip. It allowed for hope that all could still be well.

# Camera Lake

## 1

For almost a week I knew someone was filming our house at night. The first night, at the dinner table, I got a feeling in my bones. The second night, before we started eating, I peeked out the window until Judy sat down and served herself pork tenderloin. The next three nights, as we cooked and again as we cleaned up, I kept wandering to the window, as though I had business over there, and gazed out as long as possible without arousing suspicion. Finally, on Friday, I got up during dinner and Judy asked what I was doing. I told her. She said, thinking about it, that she had had a similar feeling all week. Then she stood, switched off the lights, and joined me. We cupped our hands to the glass. Both of us detected the green light of a camera, only to have it disappear when we attempted to pinpoint it, like when you focus directly on an individual star. We searched so long that when we returned to the table our venison had cooled and toughened.

"Who eats venison anyway?" I asked, poking the meat experimentally with my fork.

"You don't like it?" she asked.

"I don't know. Just who eats it? It was fine, I guess."

There was a pause. I said, "Maybe I should go out there, check it out."

She knew that I was afraid of walking out onto the ice and that I wanted her to dissuade me. We sat there at the table awhile longer eating limp asparagus.

2

This was our first winter on the lake. We moved from Philadelphia. Neither of us had ever lived outside of Pennsylvania. The house we bought was on the outskirts of a midsized town in eastern Wisconsin, which was an obvious contrast to Philly. Now we were surrounded by smiles instead of sneers, nature instead of history, and clarity instead of stimulus. All was in line with our expectations. Except we did not anticipate the distinct and unquantifiable incongruities—differences that even now I cannot articulate. Most of our conversations that first year consisted of pointing out minute and mundane details in our surroundings and contrasting them with what had always been familiar. We spent most of our time together attempting to orient ourselves.

We'd always wanted to live on a lake though and we weren't getting younger. So I got a job counseling at a prison and Judy is a massage therapist so she can work anywhere. Turned out that my getting fired was not quite a blessing in disguise, we said back then, but a welcome opportunity. When we said this, I'm almost certain we both believed it, but by the time the camera thing happened I wasn't quite sure.

In Philadelphia I had been a high school guidance counselor. My job mainly involved college advising, handing out pamphlets on teen pregnancy, and referring kids to the substance-abuse therapist. Most of the students already had their own psychologist, and I wasn't supposed to probe their inner lives—I was *told* that. That was in my job description, and I enjoyed the ordinary pleasantries of playing the middleman. The kids called me "Mr. D." They invited me to their sporting events and plays. Parents thanked me for helping their son or daughter get into college. At Christmas, people popped by my office to drop off cards and snacks and little gifts. Teachers spoke openly to me because I was supposed to be confidential and understanding, so I got all the best gossip.

But then I was fired after three students killed themselves in the same semester. All that unremarkable nicety disappeared. After that we—well, I—needed to escape. The story made the papers, and it mentioned how I had met with each of the students in the days before each tragedy. That hurt. I considered every student in that school like—well, not like my own child, but close, like a niece or nephew. To lose three of them was unbearable. We lived a couple blocks from my school, and after I was let go, I holed myself in, unable to bear the open scorn of passersby. Judy claimed not to notice the scowls, but I knew better.

Judy suggested that we move, get a fresh start, even though it must have killed a part of her to move away from Philly, where all her friends and family lived, and where she had set up an established practice. I don't think she exactly blamed me, though our situation was clearly a product of my shortcomings and confirmed beyond a doubt that I was not a gifted therapist. If I'm honest, I don't necessarily feel bad for how my actions affected her—I simply feel stupid for failing so miserably at the reasonable task of being a high school guidance counselor. I'm annoyed at myself, though I've run through it a million times in my head and am pretty sure I made no egregious mistakes. I followed every protocol. There was no talk of death or suicide, no obvious substance abuse; they weren't overly critical of themselves or preoccupied with their failures. I'm not sure that anyone in my position could have prevented what had happened. Not that I am blameless. I had the opportunity to help those kids, and while I don't believe I actively contributed to their deaths, I obviously did not do enough to save them.

The first student was referred by a teacher who expressed concerns about a dip in grades, veering her off the college path. But when the kid, Hannah, refused to speak, I babbled to fill the gaps. Allowing silence to provide space for patient introspection has always been an issue for me. Pauses make me anxious. I assume the stagnation is my fault. Since I was used to giving practical advice, I launched into my go-to career story about how I started my adult life as a roofer. I explained how day after day I'd bake up on roofs while staring at the leathery, sun-ravaged skin and twisted backs of the older guys on the crew. I described them like they were trolls. "And not even that old. Forty, forty-five," I said, then I laughed and added, "but I guess to you that's pretty old." I nodded at her, to encourage her to chuckle along with my lame joke.

In my interviews later with the school board and state counseling board I never mentioned how Hannah truly appeared to me at that moment, though I can still picture her exactly. I'd say that she wore a profoundly bored expression, except "bored" does not begin to describe it. Her face was scorched earth. She was a vortex of joy. I had worked with high schoolers for ten years and thought I had seen every manifestation of apathy and petty hatred but hers was in a different stratosphere. Still, what was I supposed to do? Refer her to a specialist because my boring story bored her too much?

I was thoroughly thrown off my game and became too depressed to finish the roofing story. The rousing conclusion usually involved how I went to school at nights to avoid turning into one of those roofers, how I even put myself through graduate school while roofing, and then I tied it all together with the idea that the very thing that I feared most and that stoked my desire for something more also funded my path out, and so I was forever grateful for being able to have been a roofer while also incredibly relieved to never again have to step foot on a boiling-hot godforsaken backbreaking roof ever again. But I did not convey that lesson to Hannah. Instead, her raw expression of pained weariness transfixed me, rendered me unable to speak another word. She forced me to grasp exactly how useless my life up until then had been and how I was kidding myself if I thought I had ever really accomplished anything. And so, without investigating the source of her malaise or delivering useful advice, I sent her away.

I did not tell the roofing story again. Even so, another student killed himself later that month. I honestly don't remember what I said to him. I only met with him briefly because he missed some application deadlines, and then later that night he took his life. After that I got the yips and could barely bring myself to speak coherently when students were in my office. I began to spout non sequiturs and trailed off in the middle of sentences. They should have removed me from the roster, but I was a counselor—I was the one who was supposed to be able to handle such burdens. Instead, I referred every student I saw to someone else. Still, there was one more—a kid with loads of potential, who could have, with a little effort, made their mark on the world. I referred this third student to the school psychologist for no real reason other than that I did not want more blood on my hands. They never made it to the appointment. I often wonder what my relationship to these deaths is on a cosmic level. As perhaps the last person they came to for help, I do feel acutely related to each of them. I consider myself to be in their debt without the means to repay. But for me, practically, it meant I was fired, and we had to leave our home of sixteen years, and, for a long time, I was unable to maintain any semblance of emotional stability. Each night for nearly two years I woke up every few hours with a knot in my chest.

And then we moved to Wisconsin, and about six months later, I started sleeping through the night. I believe this restful period began after the first major snow when, as I prepared for bed, I found myself excited to wake up, throw open the curtains, and gaze out our bedroom window at that serene, snow-covered lake. Anticipating that idyllic scene, along with the awareness that my expectations would be met, gave me hope. The camera business started around this time. I'm cognizant that the feeling of being filmed was most likely related to my newfound sense of relief—it was no coincidence that the very lake I looked forward to seeing each morning was in turn watching and recording me—yet I have never been surer of anything in my entire life. The camera was as real to me as math or when I open my palm and examine my own hand.

3

About a week after we stated our belief in the camera, Judy walked on the lake wearing snowshoes. I spotted her out there as I arrived home from work. She waved rather sheepishly when I pulled up, as though I caught her doing something childish.

"Where'd you get snowshoes?" I called to her.

"They were in the shed," she called back.

"You rascal!" I said.

I walked to her. With each step I sank ankle deep into the snow. I was always excited to be home after a day at the prison, and today I was especially glad that Judy was outside since I wanted an excuse to linger in the fading daylight and survey the lake for signs of the camera. But as I rounded the garage, I saw a man sitting on a snowmobile parked on the lake. I cursed myself for calling Judy a rascal while a stranger was within earshot. That's a funny nicknamey thing couples say when they are alone, and I was embarrassed to have said an inside joke outdoors. As I neared the shore, I noticed his snowmobile was tiger striped and his suit fire-engine red. The thought of this guy as my neighbor sapped my strength. I nodded to him.

"Say," Judy said, shifting her glance quickly to him, "do you know anything about someone filming the lake at night?"

"This lake? Who'd want to film *this* lake?" the guy said, looking around as though he might have previously missed a feature worth documenting.

"Geoff thinks someone is filming our house at night," Judy said, keeping her eyes on him. "He has a feeling."

"No," I said, with a touch of desperation. "I don't. I know they aren't. It's stupid."

"Film the actual lake?" the guy said, taking off his helmet and setting it on his lap, revealing a weathered face and thin, sweaty hair. "Can you do that at night? Night vision maybe."

"No, our house," I said. "It's stupid. Please forget about it."

Judy looked at me. "You do have this feeling though." She spoke sternly, but with a little smile, like she might be messing with this guy, or me, or both of us. She turned back to him and said, "He gets up at dinner to search for it and we keep the blinds closed all night."

I wasn't sure if I was in the middle of a prank, either as accomplice or butt, and I wished the subject would be dropped. If we kept talking about it, though, I at least wanted to point out that Judy also got up at dinner and had said she felt the same thing. It hurt that she suddenly denied belief in the camera—even if as a joke—and seemed to blame me for embroiling her in my ridiculous notion. It was now apparent that she had only joined me at the window the past couple nights out of politeness, and while I could have taken this as a supportive gesture, I was instead deeply ashamed.

"Who is it?" the guy said, concerned. His quick leap to believing such an implausible story led me to assume he was a conspiracy theorist. "Think they're filming my house? I mean, they could, I guess."

Judy shrugged and they both turned to me. I kept quiet, as I figured silence was the best strategy to get them to stop talking about it.

"Anyways," he said, dipping his head down toward Judy's snowshoes, "I was telling her how the edge of the water's the most dangerous part."

I was already uneasy that they were both on the ice, and when he said the word "dangerous," I took an extra step away from the lake.

"Figured I should come by and warn you," he added.

"I thought it was frozen solid," she said, staring at her feet.

"It is," he said. "Still, edge of the lake's the least solid."

Judy should have replied. Maybe thanked him for the potentially lifesaving advice. But she stayed silent. I was still too surprised by the snowshoes, the man's presence, and Judy ratting me out about the camera to come up with some agreeable comment to fill the void. I desperately wanted someone else to speak.

Eventually he said, "How was the venison?"

Judy only nodded. Her eyes remained firmly on the ice.

Soon after he said this, the man bade farewell and then drove disconcertingly fast toward a small bridge under which our lake connected to another lake. We watched him for about eight seconds until his snowmobile became a speck and then disappeared.

"That guy," I said when even the sound died away.

"What about him?"

"See that helmet? That getup? Think it could be him?"

"I'm not so sure anyone's out here," she said as she stomped a snow-shoe on the ice.

I gaped at her, then softened. Even then I was aware how absurd it was that we were being filmed, and yet her doubt shocked me. Had she changed her mind, or had she never actually believed in the camera in the first place? Also, who was that guy and why hadn't Judy told me that he had provided us with venison? This new development unnerved me almost as much as being filmed.

"Still," I said, "he looks like an idiot."

I talked past my loneliness that night, making sure to speak only of things I did not care about. I did not bring up the venison. I did not ask why she had treated me like a crazy person in front of a stranger, and I also didn't ask if that had all been an obscure joke. Being abandoned in my belief left me alone in the world, or at least that's how I felt during dinner.

Only later, after she fell asleep, did I creep downstairs to look out the window.

4

Somehow the prisoners found out what happened in Philly. It was bound to happen. They have a lot of time on their hands.

It surely did my reputation no favors, which was fair. Not that I'm incompetent. I've helped plenty of guys get back on their feet. A few have even called to thank me after they were released. But as soon as your character is called into question it can be tough to engage, and some inmates became more reticent than usual. I began to wonder if they believed I could kill them by talking. More likely they weren't keen on counseling in the first place and now assumed I was a lousy therapist and a child killer. Given the chance that I made anyone feel unsafe, I decided not to begin a session unless the inmate spoke first. This meant I had to learn to deal with silence.

A few of them made jokes or insinuations about Philly, but only one man, Terrence, asked me straight out. He was in his early thirties, in for a petty armed robbery—his second stint in prison. Our first couple meetings he stayed quiet. During our third meeting I kept a game of hearts up on my computer screen, thinking long and hard about each move. Hearts was my new strategy to get through the silent stretches without saying something I would later regret.

"Is it true what they say about you?" Terrence asked suddenly.

I had just gotten rid of my queen and was startled. "Excuse me?"

"You really kill those kids?" he asked.

"The kids at my old school?" I said. "No. They killed themselves. I was just their counselor."

"Right," Terrence said, as though I confirmed what he said.

"I'm sorry?" I asked.

"Okay, so you didn't kill them kill them, like you didn't slit their throats, but you must have said *something* to make them do it, right? Some kind of Hannibal Lecter shit?"

"Not necessarily," I said, a little defensively. "Kids have all kinds of pressures. And you know, you don't have to worry about anything when you're talking with me. It's absolutely impossible that—"

"But what did you *say*?"

"I don't know," I said. "No. Well, I told the first one about how I became a guidance counselor."

I told him the roofing story. Really it pertains to inmates better than high schoolers since there's no doubt that being a counselor is a step up for them. I concluded by saying, "I realized the other day that I'm the same age as those older guys were back then. And look"—I showed him my hands—"hands are callus-free, no back pain, and I don't have skin cancer."

Telling the story felt good, an unburdening. I saw that it was just a harmless, tedious anecdote. Also, I did recently realize that I was the same age as those older roofers, but I chose not to share the observation with Judy, so I was glad for the opportunity to tell someone. I held up my soft hands for too long, twisted them palm-to-back for us both to admire.

"Man, you didn't kill anybody," he said, annoyed.

"I know. That's what I've been saying." I put my hands down.

"Lame-ass story."

"Did you want me to have killed someone?" I said. "Isn't it better that I didn't?"

"Shit, I don't know."

"No, it would be better, for you, if I had, right?" I said. "It's more interesting if that ability exists and if you're in the presence of it. My having killed someone adds some intrigue and danger to these meetings, right?"

"Dude's just talking," Terrence said, rolling his eyes.

I wanted to continue, to explain, but our time was up.

5

That evening I pulled into the driveway and then turned so the headlights shined onto the lake. I wanted to see if anyone was filming. I searched alone now, instead of at dinner, and I no longer talked about the camera with Judy. But my faith was as strong as ever. The previous night while taking out the garbage, I heard someone cough out there and I wasn't surprised at all, only satisfied to receive confirmation.

As I peered out my windshield, Judy opened the door and got in.

"Wasn't sure you got my texts," she said, shivering and stamping snow off her shoes and onto the passenger-side floor mat.

I looked at my phone and saw there were three new texts.

"Yep," I said, my voice higher pitched than usual.

"You know which is his house?" she asked.

"House?"

"Stan's. For dinner."

I pulled out and started driving. It felt good to be taking a trip together, even if I had no clue where I was going.

"Stan just stopped by this afternoon and asked us over," she said. "I couldn't think of a reason to say no. It's tough to turn someone down when they're standing right in front of you."

"Wait a minute, who's Stan?" I asked.

"Our neighbor. Snowmobile guy," she said.

"Jesus. Him?"

"It would have been rude to say no after he gave us all that venison," she said. "Where did you think we were going?"

The secret venison still bothered me. How could she not have mentioned that some weirdo in a bright-red suit rode over on his snowmobile and handed her a bunch of venison? It should have been a running joke between us. Instead, I felt cut out. To be fair, it may have freaked her out to realize she now lived in a place where it's normal for people to hand you venison for no good reason. Like how I hadn't told her that the prisoners figured out what happened in Philly simply because I didn't want to think about it more than was necessary. If I had been honest with her, I would have explained how my talk with Terrence left me shaky and depressed and that maybe this wasn't the ideal evening for socializing.

Stan served us stew. Possibly venison stew—I never asked. I won't pretend I wasn't wary of Stan for showing up at our house so often while I was out, but he turned out to be an affable, quiet guy. I would not call him bright. He was easy. I understood why Judy accepted both the venison and the invitation. The stew was peppery and delicious.

Though I no longer had issues with Stan, and despite constantly interacting with people at work, I found I was socially off my game. Not that Stan noticed or cared, but it was highly unusual for me to be distracted in this situation. Dinners like this were my specialty. My need to dispel silence was a godsend around shy people. Now I was hot and short of breath. I find that it helps to expose the root of anxiety, so I examined what was wrong, and discovered that my attention was diverted by Terrence's question from earlier in the day: "But what did you *say*?" It was, I realized, the first time anyone had directly accused me of killing my students on purpose.

I chugged the wine we brought as quickly as politeness allowed. Despite my choking angst, I had managed to thus far carry the conversation like I was a cruise ship director. At one point I said, "Boy it's cold. Bet you've seen some winters up here, huh, Stan?" And I continued to internally panic as he regaled us with stories of notable winters past. Soon, however, Stan cut through my bullshit.

"You okay there, Geoff?" he asked in a concerned and friendly way. "That stew hitting you wrong?"

I checked myself, wondered what gave me away. Judy and I had held frequent, brief eye contact during Stan's stories, but she had given no indication that I appeared unwell. No matter my outward symptoms, though, I was caught, and grateful for Stan having taken notice. His guilelessness appealed to me, and I was tipsy enough to share something intimate.

"Honestly, Stan, it's been a tough couple of years," I said. The words came out of me as though released from a cage.

I told Stan what happened at my old school. This appeared to be more than he had bargained for, but he hung in there and nodded along sympathetically, though I could tell by the way he glanced at his empty bottle that he wanted to get up and grab another beer.

"It wasn't his fault," Judy said in my defense. "They're kids. Cyberbullying and hormones. They don't have a chance."

"It's never easy," Stan said.

"What do you do, Stan? For work," I asked. Admitting my nervousness calmed me, but I saw no reason to dwell on my past, especially since further discussion could revive my agitation.

"Construction in the summer. Unemployment now," Stan said.

Judy smiled at him and then me. "So, we're *both* out of work."

"You know I used to roof, Stan?" I asked, changing the subject again.

Stan was at the refrigerator grabbing a round of beers. He shook his head and laughed for some reason.

"I hated it—the heat, the heights," I said. I felt a reckless need to indulge, and plunged back in. "Funny thing is, when that stuff with the kids was going down, all I could think was how after I was fired, I'd have to go back to roofing. After the second one I was scared shitless that I was one kid away from being a roofer."

"He was a scapegoat," Judy said to Stan. "It's not like anyone thought he actually did anything wrong. The kids loved him. He got a very nice severance package."

"But Stan"—I looked him straight in the eye, my face burned—"I constantly thought how I was one kid away from going back to roofing. It scared the hell out of me, but I also craved it, like the punishment could absolve me. That's messed up, right?"

I had never said any of this to Judy, so I avoided looking at her, which meant I trained my eyes on poor Stan, who fiddled with his beer label. Of course, it's easier to confess to a disinterested third party—that's the basis of therapy. And though it was awkward to drop this on some guy I just met, I also had quite a bit to drink. I was remarkably calm and allowed the ensuing silence to linger. Crazily I hoped that someone would ask, "But what did you *say*?"

After a minute, Judy pointed at a painting of a stout man in a black bowler hat and asked, "Who's that?"

"I don't know," Stan said. "Just liked the picture."

The moment passed without comment on my admission, and with its passing, my unease returned. To cover my distress, I resumed my cruise director role and said, "This place is snug as hell, Stan. What do you do for heat?" And so, as we finished our stew and drinks, Stan went into detail about his stove and how he cuts his own wood with a mechanized chopper.

Later, as we readied to leave, Stan remembered something and held up a finger. He dashed to a back room, we heard rummaging, and he ran back in, proudly holding up a black disk.

"The hell's that?" I asked, though I knew. I felt myself pale.

"I'm no expert, but . . ." He trailed off as he handed me a lens cap.

"Where'd you find it?" I asked.

"Edge of the lake. Way out. Over by the bait and tackle on the west end. Still, interesting, right? Think it's *them*?" He nodded earnestly as he spoke.

I appreciated his belief but was too overwhelmed by the physical evidence to speak. Judy thanked him for a pleasant evening and opened the door. Stan's gesture—especially how he sprinted back to his room like that, his boots clomping on the wood floor—was touching. I hoped my warm handshake and eye contact conveyed my gratitude.

About halfway home I stopped examining the lens cap and placed it on the dashboard. Almost immediately, Judy snatched it up, lowered her window, and dropped it out.

6

The next day I was in my office with a headache, mulling over the lens cap development as well as contemplating the merits of calling Terrence back in to see if he had any further accusations. In my current state the two events seemed somehow connected.

There was a knock on my door.

The rehabilitation specialist on duty poked his head in and told me an inmate died by suicide last night.

"Was it Terrence?" I asked instinctively.

"Which Terrence?" he asked.

I shook my head and said to forget it. I affirmed that nobody I spoke to had displayed warning signs, and then we briefly discussed how this would affect our day. Unfortunately, such deaths are alarmingly common in prisons, so the protocols were in place, though this was the first death by suicide since I arrived.

When he closed my door, panic overtook me. Luckily, I suppose, my experiences in Philadelphia had prepared me for such attacks. For about fifteen minutes I had to simply accept that chemicals were coursing through my body that made me feel as though I was dying a lonely and painful death.

I did not call Judy while this happened. There was no reason to worry her. Plus, if this indicated another upheaval, she might get her hopes up that she will soon move back home. I could, after all, be a roofer in Philly as easily as anywhere else.

Once I sufficiently recovered, I got back to work. Still, I could not shake the feeling I was responsible, though the man who killed himself had not been in my care. Perhaps, I thought nonsensically, Terrence told the man my roofing story. I looked down at my soft hands and saw them as an indictment—the hands of a killer. I imagined myself as I otherwise would have been, with leathery skin and constant back pain, but strong and capable and responsible for building roofs that kept people safe.

Around three I got a call from a chiropractor named Dr. Hammer. Apparently, Judy gave my number as an alternate contact, and she had not answered her phone. He asked me to pass along the message that a room would be available for her next week. A room? He said a room in his office, to give massages, so they could share clients. I said I would tell her the good news.

The call both cheered and frightened me. Judy would be thrilled to go back to work, to be a part of our new community, to have renewed purpose. Our life was back on track, and this time I could not afford to take it for granted. This most recent death was a reminder of how quickly peace of mind can be stolen away by circumstances outside of our control. How we don't always consider the systems by which everyone is connected and watched over. How our collective responsibility for each other exists even if not in the ways we intend or imagine. Maybe a camera on me was a good thing. Maybe it showed that I had no ill intentions. Maybe it was proof of my innocence.

I looked up Dr. Hammer online and was only momentarily dismayed that he was roughly my age and had no obvious facial deformities. I searched some more to figure out if he was perhaps gay but found no definitive proof either way. After about a half hour I stopped typing and lifted my hands above my head as though to prove I was unarmed. I had to let this go. I wouldn't ruin her moment. It was outside of my control.

7

That night we celebrated Judy's partnership with Dr. Hammer by eating at the Chinese place in town. We drank a bottle of wine with dinner and every time we refilled our glasses, I toasted her. I didn't tell her about the suicide at the prison. I chose instead to bury that fear and pain deep inside myself, which allowed me to be genuinely happy for her success.

At home we switched to drinking Manhattans. When we eventually stumbled upstairs, Judy went to close the curtains and I said, "Why?" She smiled and left them open.

Later, when Judy was asleep, I dressed and went outside to the shed. The people we bought the house from left all kinds of junk in there, like those old snowshoes Judy enjoyed horsing around with. But the thought of walking out onto the ice, especially in the dark, prickled my palms. Instead, I grabbed a rickety stepladder.

It's unwise to stand atop a snowy roof, particularly one as peaked as ours, and especially after consuming as much alcohol as I had that night. And yet there I was. I had long ago promised myself that I would never step upon another roof, and this was indeed the first one I had mounted since my roofer days. Well, I thought, who cares what I had promised myself? It's just a roof.

I shuffled up higher, until the entire lake was in view. Deathly quiet. Half moon behind clouds. The darkness tricked my vision as I searched for the camera, so I anchored myself into the snow as I waved both hands above my head and yelled, "You out there?"

It was the first time I had reached out to the camera, and indulging in the absurdity made me chuckle, at least until a voice called back, "Get down from there, you'll break your neck!"

Someone was probably out on a late-night hike. Or it was my own voice echoed back. Or Stan was messing with me. Or I was drunk and heard what I wanted to hear. Whatever. It doesn't matter. Point is that out there I was exhilarated. I stood and cupped my hands like a megaphone to shout back, but before I could speak, my foot slipped. I caught myself and realized I had to listen to the cameraperson. It was icy as hell up there. If I fell, I would die.

## 8

The next day I again had a headache, but a pleasant one because it was the weekend, and I was able to lounge around while Judy prepared for her first day at Dr. Hammer's. I made no mention of what happened up on the roof. Though it was part of the reason for my cheeriness, it would have ruined her good mood.

"We should go up on the roof a bunch this summer," I said to her while she worked, and I reclined on the couch. "Set chairs up and drink wine while staring at the lake."

She finished typing something. "Why will you go up on the roof, but you're afraid of the ice? The roof is just as dangerous."

I had never considered this. "I've been on a lot of roofs," I said. "The only association I have with frozen lakes is people falling through."

She turned back to her screen and said, "We're going to live here for a long time, you know."

This made me happy. Before I could reply, I heard the roar of an engine outside.

"That must be Stan," Judy said. She then anticipated my question. "I asked him to come over. You need something to do."

I laughed because it was a funny way of telling me that my jolly boredom was annoying. Then I groaned because hanging out with Stan sounded uncomfortable. I was too hungover to force conversation.

"I didn't ask you because you would have said no," she added, anticipating my next question. "But I want you off that couch. I'd like to work without interruptions. Besides, it would be nice if you had a friend around here."

Stan hailed us from outside and Judy shooed me off. He was in his crazy outfit and waved a mittened hand while remaining seated on his snowmobile. On the seat behind him was a second helmet. "You still think someone's videotaping your house?" he called out over the engine.

I nodded and laughed.

"Want to go look?" he asked.

"Of course not!" I said, smiling.

"The hell not? Come on. I got an extra suit." I could tell he was excited. "It's going to be dark soon. We can catch them in the act."

My smile dropped when I understood he was serious. "The ice? It can't support both of us on that thing."

"That ice could hold up a house," he said.

"He'd love to go," Judy said from behind me. "Thank you for the generous offer, Stan!"

## 9

I found myself skimming over the ice on Stan's death machine, searching for a camera that could not possibly exist, though I was so afraid that I kept my eyes tightly shut. If I were counseling myself at that moment, I would ask from where my fear stemmed. My answer would be: dying. Freezing, helpless, drowning nothingness.

The therapist me would ask: Do you think Stan is unaware of the risks? Do you think he has a death wish or wishes you harm? My answer: Of course not, no.

Great, so my fear was baseless, but it was still fear. Bad patient that I was, what I most wanted was to stop riding and to go home. We were too heavy and going too fast. Maybe Stan miscalculated the risks. I decided to tap Stan on the shoulder and order him to take me back. I opened my eyes, only to discover that my visor was completely fogged over. Though still frozen by fear and now disconcerted by my sudden blindness, I managed to flip the visor up. Wind and snow whipped my eyes as I peered into the darkness. My vision cleared, and before I could speak, I saw a light out of the corner of my eye.

"There it is!" I yelled. Forgetting how terrified I was, I pounded Stan's shoulder and pointed at the twinkling green dot.

He swerved the machine, and the headlight reflected the lens of a camera mounted above the spindly legs of a tripod.

I pumped my fist in victory, but Stan interrupted.

"Just a little doe," he said, and cut the engine. "Hunters probably got her mama."

Indeed, it was the shining eyes of a mesmerized deer.

What followed was a silence so absolute that it was difficult to consider it silence at all. Indeed, I had not experienced such an expectant hush since I told Hannah my roofing story. I held my breath to keep the deer from bolting and thought how if I had done this at the school, Hannah might still be alive. I should have allowed silence to breed analysis. But back then I had considered my own discomfort to be of greater importance than hers and so failed to take advantage of the moment. It was a mistake caused by my shortcomings, and there was no way now to fix it.

"All alone out here," Stan whispered. "She won't make it through the winter."

If I were a different person, or if I were telling a different story, I would have attempted some futile gesture to save the fawn and make spiritual amends. Instead, as I kept quiet and continued to hold my breath, my thoughts shifted to Judy and Stan's secret venison, which, for all I knew, may have been this little deer's mother. I decided that I had been right to keep my concerns about the venison to myself. Too much of my life was spent worrying about things that did not matter, or that I was powerless to change. My job was to not to make the same mistake twice.

I needed to breathe, and so finally exhaled.

At the sound of my breath, the fawn snapped out of it and leapt into the darkness. I climbed off the snowmobile and stood on the ice.

# Props

He had taken to watching his son sleep. This, he knew, was the action of a creepy man, or at best of a more doting father than he could credit himself to be. But lately he had been restless and the darkness, the teenaged breathing, calmed him. Lurking at the kid's bedside forced him to regulate his movements and allowed him the patience to lie in wait for night sounds he would otherwise never catch. Heels snapped against the sidewalk. A muscle car engine gunned. Raccoons rustled through human leavings. A brass band rendition of the national anthem played in the distance.

His son was sixteen, too old to be watched sleeping, so he took pains to remain undetected and left after a couple hours. The routine had little to do with his son—he was not gazing in wonder at the boy's features, nor was he enthralled by the young man his son had become. He stood there only to expose himself to the darkness and those night sounds. His son's role was to up the stakes. Besides the potential damage to the boy's psyche, witnessing his father's looming presence might well kibosh their already tenuous relationship.

Lately he had needed to be propped up, and so he stood in his son's room when the kid stayed over. His own mother, he believed, required similar buttressing when she was his age. Given the genetic connection, he assumed the source of their malaise was chemical. Or maybe, back when he was a child, he had projected his own frailties onto her. She never asked for his assistance. He simply thought he could read her, and so he entertained her by dancing as she did the dishes, performing impromptu plays while she ironed the laundry, or giving the dog piano lessons when she was not up to cooking dinner. So far, he had refrained from asking his children to prop him—first off, they wouldn't, but even if they obliged, he could not imagine so nakedly revealing himself. Instead, he watched the boy sleep, listened to the night sounds, went to bed, woke tired, dragged himself to work. Always tired.

Living in this world as currently constructed made him restless. Stopping on the way home from work to watch some kids play basketball only took up so much of his time. He would like to be an alcoholic, to tell the truth.

Not dissatisfied. Restless. It's different.

He used to have a pal. Mario. They worked together second shift at a warehouse. Neither of them had a car and so they walked home together.

They would get out of work at midnight, go across the street, buy a twelve-pack of beer, tear it open, and hide six each all over themselves. In coat pockets, each sleeve. They started buying clothes specifically for the purpose—cargo pants, for example. They walked home drinking one after another for about three miles. Their clothes emptied as they went along, and they felt themselves lighten. Mario lived closer and they would stop at his place, eat a frozen pizza, play some spades, watch the Military Channel. They made sure not to wake up Mario's wife.

They each enjoyed this walk home more than they could admit, and often clocked the time during their shift, not anticipating the end of the workday, but looking forward to walking home, joking around, telling stories, drinking beer that warmed against their bodies as they went along. They both felt like they were getting away with a transgression and never told their significant others about their post-work routine.

He got moved to first shift. Everyone put in for first shift because a normal schedule was what you were supposed to want. Mario stayed on second shift, though he had seniority, and everyone assumed, correctly, that the modified priority was due to race, since Mario was Black. When the manager informed him of the shift change, he hesitated, but the only reason to turn down the opportunity was the afterwork walks with Mario and, when he thought of it this way, it was obviously silly to alter his entire life to indulge his commute. Might even mar the ritual if he chose to do it. Might come to expect more of it. Might soon regret not taking advantage of his good fortune. Mario might even be next in line to gain the first shift. Then where would he be? Walking three miles home alone in the dark, that's where.

From then on, he only saw Mario when Mario clocked in as he clocked out. They nodded and both knew what they had lost. Now he took the bus home because they were still running that early in the day; he'd be home in twenty minutes, and his wife would be awake. Later, after they broke up and he had nobody to talk to after work, he recognized that seeing her upon his return had been nearly ideal. He had been unable to appreciate spending more time with her simply because he compared it unfavorably to walking home with Mario.

Back in his second-shift days, he would get home at about two in the morning after his jolly commute, half-drunk, and either spoon her sleeping body for a half hour or so, or else she'd be asleep in a chair in a failed attempt to wait up for him. Such effort was rare and should have been cherished, he later admitted. In those Mario days he stayed up until almost dawn every night watching recorded basketball games, or late-night movies on TNT, or he went up on the roof and searched for people climbing out of windows, or he fed the spiders in the basement with crickets he bought from the pet store. He saw his wife in the afternoons, ate breakfast. Five thirty though. Every evening. She never would have said it, but she preferred him working second shift too. The effort to make the most of their abbreviated time was better than having hours to waste.

Rest of the story makes sense. He started stopping at Mario's after work, even though Mario wasn't home. For old time's sake. He had met

Mario's wife a couple times when Mario had fallen asleep. Mario dozed off in his recliner once, twice a week while they watched some program about the bombing of Dresden or whatever. It was stimulating to be in another person's house when he thought nobody was awake. He went around flipping switches, opening drawers, looking in closets, in the garbage. Turned on the tap to see how long it took for their hot water to kick in. Harmless stuff. Once he accidentally turned on the garbage disposal and it woke her because there was a fork down there and it made a godawful noise. By the time she came out in her nightie and asked what he was doing, he had moved on to the stove, was on his back looking for the pilot light, because his was electric. He told her he was just figuring out how things worked. She was unperturbed.

The first time that he went over there when Mario wasn't around, he stood in the doorway while Mario's wife stared at him from inside the screen door. He hadn't been over there for a few months, and it took her a minute to figure out who he was. He had since grown a beard. He said, "I used to come by with Mario. After work." She let him in. It took the sting out of the loss of his and Mario's commute. But in all honesty, he would rather have those times walking home with Mario than the times with his wife. That's if he had to choose which times he was able to keep.

Both Mario's wife and his own wife became pregnant at the same time. Wasn't tough for Mario to guess what went on. His own wife found out because Mario went out of his way to tell her, and now both kids visited on the same weekends and the half siblings had indeed become close friends. Taken at sum total, an agreeable outcome. He had welcomed the births, and even if they now mostly lived elsewhere, having kids was a task, and gave him events to attend. Everyone looked forward to the weekends they stayed over. Marked the time.

He started to watch his son sleep not long after being informed of Mario's present whereabouts. This knowledge came about by chance. He had called in an HVAC guy to inspect the ducts, and it turned out this HVAC guy and Mario worked together. Imagine, if he'd set the appointment for a different day, Mario himself might have come over. The duct guy said that Mario had a new house, a new wife, and new kids.

"All set up," he replied.

"He sure is," this HVAC guy said, and then added, "Nice guy."

So, he decided to reach out to Mario for the first time in sixteen, seventeen years. The peaceful vigil at his son's bedside triggered a desire to reconnect, made him believe that reconciliation was probable. Passing time with another person in a darkened setting made him itch to see his old friend. Admittedly, the idea of going to visit Mario at work had not occurred to him while he stood over his slumbering progeny. In the dark it was all he could do to keep still and silent enough to not wake the boy so he could hear those night sounds.

He went over to the HVAC place to wait Mario out, though he figured he was not welcome. Thought it was worth a chance. Without a word Mario walked right up and punched him clean in the face. After taking the punch, he picked up the twelve-pack sitting at his feet and asked if Mario would like to have a beer, take a walk like old times, maybe drink themselves all the way over to Mario's new house. Mario said, in so many words, that those days are over and can never come back again.

As they walked their separate ways, he thought how once a light the color of applesauce hovered over his son's bed, and that he used to witness a similar phenomenon in those second-shift days with Mario, in the big fluorescent lights above the warehouse parking lot. There, the bugs swarmed so thick around those big lot lamps that they took on an applesauce color and consistency. He was not sure why it had happened in his boy's room. Probably a trick of the light.

His jaw hurt, and to sharpen the pain, he rubbed the spot where Mario had connected. He thought about how he watched his son sleep, picked up hitchhikers, watched basketball, slept with his friends' wives. He worked, he slept, he ate. Once on an Indian reservation he ate a possum. His brother called, his kids canceled their weekends, his ex-wife stopped by drunk. TV. When the car requires maintenance, he feels a little excited. He tried to get into the internet but that depressed him more than he could express. He goes to the dentist. On the news they said a comet was coming close to Earth and he forgot to go outside and search the night sky. A man once threatened to gut him in the street and take his shoes. He knew that coaxial connections were a thing but was also aware that he will die without understanding their function. His son once asked him about Punnet squares. He bought shorts without trying them on and they were too short. Repaved the driveway. At a department store he saw the sports guy from the local news playing the sample video games they have set up there. There was a wig in the street, run over by a bunch of cars, and he stepped on it. He was once disturbed from sleep by an earthquake. About twice per winter, this is when there's snow, late at night, he'll gaze out his window and be convinced that it is the saddest thing he will ever see. At a movie, alone, he became convinced he was dying of a heart attack, and so he leaned over in his seat so that, if he fell dead, he would land in the aisle, and someone would notice his lifeless body before the closing credits. Light bulb replacement. Moths once ate the clothes in the back of his closet, and he felt relief. Stove noises. Every so often a woman came into his life, and he could not imagine life without her. He got a wart removed. It grew back. If it came down to it, he did not think he would mind much if his house burned down. He falls asleep in front of the TV. TV.

His mother didn't have this much. She had him. Back then he was happy to entertain her.

He never went back to Mario's work and found a new HVAC guy. He never brought any of this up to his kids. They did not ask about the bruise on his jaw, and he did not offer an explanation. Got a good laugh when he told the story at work though. Might as well try to make it all a good time.

It's difficult to get other people to sustain you. They need to be around. His son remained unaware he had been watched as he slept. The practice ceased after the Mario business, but it might well be resumed if necessary.

No, that time was over and should never come back again. The stakes were too high. He did not want to dissuade his children from inhabiting the orbit of people who make them happy. They needed to be left out of this. What he needed was to prop himself, even if sometimes it's like putting a chair under a door handle, where it seems destined to slip but holds back almost anything from coming in.

# GLASS MONKEY

## 1

We never learned why my mom had been brought home in a police car. She was not the type to run into trouble with the law. As far as we knew, she didn't drink or smoke or do much of anything except work and look after us. Perhaps the riskiest move she had ever made was to marry my father, though in 1967, when they were married, he didn't look like a gamble. In their wedding picture, at least, he appears decent and normal in his army uniform. The only hint of his misalignment in that photograph is that one eye is slightly closed, as though squinting, like he's baffled that people chose to attend a wedding. I was his youngest daughter, and he used to give me that same confused squint. I imagined he was trying to figure out why I was so often in his sight.

By the summer of 1987, when my mother was driven home by the police, I was eleven and my father had unexpectedly and without explanation quit his job to spend more time in the basement. Doing what, we did not know. We saw no fruits of any labor. My mother worked two jobs and, even the evening after her famous ride, always made us dinner.

A lack of clues did not keep my older siblings from speculating. They seemed to hope she had done something exciting. Maybe, my brother Keith said, she's working undercover, and they dropped her off after a bust. Or maybe, my sister, Linda, chimed in, she was giving evidence against her boss, whom we all assumed was a crook because he had a mustache and a gold tooth. My brother Steve did not allow for bravery. Knowing it upset me, he rattled off everything that I did not want to imagine my mother doing. He said she embezzled money. He said she was a kleptomaniac. He said she was a junkie and did heroin under a bridge. I ran from the room crying.

## 2

To ease the pressure on my mom, it was decided that we would be individually shipped to various aunts and uncles that summer. I believe my father came up with this solution to solve the problem of my mother. I was allowed no input, though I would have been in favor.

Now, decades later, my being sent to Aunt Elaine's has become a family joke. It's one of many often-told stories that help us make sense of our childhoods as well as own up to and make fun of our past deviant or embarrassing choices—or, in my case, to compartmentalize our dad's disregard for our welfare and our mother's exhaustion, which had allowed for dangerously poor judgment. We laugh about the time Keith flipped his Toyota Corolla and crawled out from the wreckage unscathed. We cringe talking about when Bobby grew a mullet, started chewing tobacco, and dressed like Axl Rose, which we have dubbed his "summer hick" phase. We shake our heads when Steve tells the details of how he was caught stealing a Brewers jersey from the mall and my mom had to leave work to pick him up. And we smirk and widen our eyes, stupefied that our parents sent me to Aunt Elaine's.

I would never say this to my siblings because we don't get together often enough to dampen the mood with heavy emotions, but I still resent my mom for making me go on that trip, even if I have come to believe it was not necessarily her fault. While I think I understand why she permitted it, what I can't get over is that I was the only child who was put in danger, though, as the youngest, I was the least equipped to take care of myself. From then on, and to this day, I cannot help but wonder if she loved me less than the others.

But at the time I was excited to go to my aunt's house. I had never traveled alone, and I saw it as an opportunity to receive undivided attention. Back then I considered adult relatives to be mere vehicles for my enjoyment. To me, Elaine was simply one of many aunts who swanned into and out of summer vacations. Her main feature, in my mind, was that she lived in Elkhart Lake, where I was told there would be a boat race. This held a death-defying appeal for me ever since I saw a speedboat catch an air current, spin backward, and explode into the water on *The Wide World of Sports.*

My cousin Denise called a week before I was to leave and offered to drive me. To my mind, this seemed natural. Only later did I realize that no twenty-one-year-old college student chooses to take a trip with their eleven-year-old cousin to see their weird aunt in some lame resort town. I never asked why she came along, though no matter her intention, I'm grateful she did. All I cared about back then was that I got to hang out with my coolest cousin.

### 3

My Aunt Elaine lived in a townhouse behind a golf course. I had heard my mom say once that all divorced women lived in townhouses. When we arrived, I thought it was cozy and far from depressing. I was only disappointed because I assumed, since she lived in the town of Elkhart Lake, that the lake was right outside her door. It turned out to be miles away.

Denise parked, smiled at me, and said, "Stay close to me this week, okay? No matter what, make sure I'm around. It's fine, just, you know. Aunt Elaine." I didn't know, so I nodded absently and pulled the door handle. Before I could get out, though, she grabbed my arm so hard it hurt, looked me in the eyes, and said, "I'm serious." Nobody had ever spoken to me with such intensity or inflicted pain upon me for my own good. I lacked the tools to decipher her meaning, and so only registered fright at the pain and assumed I had made a mistake.

My aunt answered the door wearing a shiny blue Adidas tracksuit. For some reason she stood in the doorway and made us wait outside like we were a pair of Jehovah's Witnesses. I had never seen a grown woman wear a tracksuit for no reason, and I thought she looked amazing. Denise's painful warning had unsettled me but left me more angry at Denise than wary of Elaine and, without thinking, but probably seeking connection, I reached out and stroked Elaine's shiny material, touching my fingertips to the pant leg.

Elaine regarded this action silently—I was focused on her leg and so did not see her expression, though I assume it was somewhere between indifferent and puzzled—and when I glanced up, I saw she was facing Denise, who stared off to the side with measured nonchalance through her aviator sunglasses. Denise made it clear that she was more interested in the man mowing the lawn next door than she was in her aunt.

"Look who's here," Elaine said, smiling ironically at Denise. "It's Fonzie in his cool shades. No sun inside, you know."

"Hi, Elaine," Denise said drily, keeping her focus on the lawn mower. "You're looking tan."

I refocused on my aunt. Indeed, she was brown and wrinkled as a roasted pecan.

Elaine grinned and nodded with raised eyebrows, a look I took to be an adult conveying comprehension of an inappropriate inside joke.

"What's this one doing?" Elaine said, speaking to Denise as she nodded at me.

Denise shrugged and guided my hand away from Elaine's pants.

Elaine bent down to my level. "How's your dad?"

"Hi, Aunt Elaine," I said. It hit me that she had asked a question. "I think he's good."

"I'll *bet*," she said, rolling her eyes to Denise, seemingly to convey privileged information, before she turned back to me. "You looking forward to this weekend?"

They both stared at me, though obviously they did not care what I had to say. Put on the spot, I nodded shyly. I recognized that I was supposed to play the role of the enthusiastic youngster, but after Denise's warning and the weirdly charged atmosphere since Elaine opened the door, I found that my dominant emotion was low-level obstinate anger. I could not stand the way Elaine addressed me—her voice was phony and sarcastic as though she was addressing a pet iguana. Instead of being doted on, or a part of things, they treated me as an obligation. I suddenly wished Denise had not come. Her presence skewed and diverted the attention I craved. I decided to say some witty, cutting remark so I could join in, but by the time something came to mind, Elaine had already disappeared into the house.

4

Inside, the house was dark as a cave. Dim even after my eyes adjusted. Lining the walls of the living room were framed posters of far-off places with the location printed at the bottom: "Morocco" or "The Pubs of Ireland" or "Hard Rock Café: Tokyo." Foreign-looking objects like tiki heads, stone soldiers, and colorful knitted dolls cluttered the shelves and tabletops.

Back then I was impressed. Her experience intimidated me. The houses I frequented as a child were filled with items bought simply to fill the space, and any framed pictures were of the home's inhabitants, as though they needed to be reminded that their bodies existed. I admit that there is a part of me, now, that cannot help but believe Elaine's tacky souvenirs and posters marked her as a sad and lonely failure who needed to point to the remnants of a vacation and say, "That's me," to prove her full life. This part of me sees those displayed acquisitions as physical manifestations of her empty inner life. But the logical part of myself—the part I believe in, the part that is not afraid of being seen as a lame midwesterner with bad taste, the part that does not need to make fun of things to prove my own correctness and sophistication— believes Elaine was brave in her loneliness and that traveling solo was an attempt to orient herself in the wider world, or even to briefly escape the systemic obstacles that blocked her chances at happiness. My own mother, for example, surely thought that being without a child was one of Elaine's many faults. I respect that Elaine allowed vulgarity to provide the evidence that she was more than a divorced woman living alone in a townhouse.

"Wine coolers in the fridge," Elaine called to us.

Denise led the way. As we moved through the house, I noticed cigarette butts everywhere. In ashtrays, lips of beer cans, stubbed into a half-empty pudding container. The mess indicated insecurity, and I suddenly felt dangerously adrift. To offset the homesickness that began to clench my stomach, I imagined myself in the comfort of my own living room reporting back to my siblings on the hilarious disarray of Elaine's life. The contextualization of the mess—taking control of it by making my observations into a private joke—gave me courage, or perhaps made me feel I was superior to my surroundings and so had nothing to fear.

Elaine rushed into the kitchen. Broomstick thin under her tracksuit, her hair roughly the thickness of silk filaments and obviously curled by curlers. Pretty in a way, except she was shaped like a candy apple and far too tan. She flipped on the light and touched the crown of my head as she passed. Her fingernails tickled my scalp and sent a shiver down my back, which raised my spirits and made me giggle. She rummaged in the refrigerator and emerged with an Old Style and a wine cooler. She placed the wine cooler in front of me. "Get some sun?" she said.

Denise, who had already downed half her own wine cooler, said, "No."

"What?" Elaine said, feigning confusion.

Denise indicated the wine cooler.

"Oh, just one. You did at her age," Elaine said.

Denise sighed and put it back in the fridge.

"Look at you!" Elaine said, smirking. "So responsible." She winked and, eyeing Denise but addressing me, added, "I'll give you some sips off my Style."

Each townhouse in the complex had a square of concrete behind it, which Elaine dubbed "the patio." The others were adorned with little useless fences and hanging flowers. One was lined with towering sunflowers.

Elaine's had two plastic deck chairs, the kind that sank when you sat in them, and a clay pot that was overfilled with cigarette butts. They lounged on the folding chairs, and I sat cross-legged on the concrete. Every so often I grunted in whiny protest at this unfair arrangement. Nobody seemed to know what to say.

The early highlight of our time on the patio was when we watched an old golfer practice at a tee box about thirty yards away until, just as he was about to swing, his golf bag slowly tipped over and clubs and balls spilled everywhere. We got a kick out of that. As the guy bent down to pick up his gear, Elaine—for some reason—said, "Serves him right."

I was thirsty, but worried I'd be forced to drink a wine cooler if I spoke up. Instead, I sat in the blazing sun with a dry mouth and stared at a golf course. Elaine was apparently uninterested in forcing conversation, and Denise only sucked at her wine cooler and perhaps dozed off at some point. The silence was unbearable, but though I was naturally chatty, I couldn't bring myself to speak. I blame it on my older brothers, who had around this time begun playing a game at my expense where they would encourage me to talk about myself by asking me about my friends or what I did at recess, and as I spoke, they would hold eye contact and nod along, and then they would eagerly urge me on by saying, "That's so *interesting*! Tell me more." Of course, as soon as I continued my story they'd walk away laughing. By the time I arrived at Elaine's, my brothers had managed to convince me that everything I had to say was hysterically dull.

So, out on the patio, I forced myself to come up with interesting conversation, and soon recalled that I was sitting there in the hot sun dirtying my jean shorts because my mother had been brought home in a police car. I had no idea if Elaine and Denise were unaware or if they had so far avoided the topic for my sake, but either way I became excited at the prospect of taking on the role of entertainer and disseminator of gossip. I rehearsed what I would say, crafted my opening and the general outline of events—this was a strategy I had lately taught myself because I became overexcited on the rare instances when I was the center of attention—but when I imagined telling the story, I felt only sadness. I pictured the look on my mom's face while she waited for the cop to come back and open the door for her, though I hadn't actually seen her arrive. If I were a different person, and if my aunt and cousin were different people, perhaps I could have discussed my deep-rooted shame with them, worked myself out of the spiderweb of feelings in which I was caught. Instead, I stayed quiet, which was the best that I could do under the circumstances.

"How about you get us another round, Linda?" Elaine said.

"Karen," Denise corrected sleepily.

Inside, I discovered that the refrigerator held mayonnaise, alcohol, a couple of greased-through KFC boxes, and a single desiccated orange. I closed the door and drank water from the tap, washed the sun off my face.

The house was air-conditioned, so I lingered. An odd sensation, to want to be alone. I wasn't the type of child who had secret hiding places or read under the stairs. I tagged along a block behind my brothers hoping they would ask me to join their baseball game, or I'd quietly fidget on my sister's bed while she read, or I'd hang at my mother's skirt until she invented reasons to force me from the kitchen. Suddenly, I preferred the cool dimness of the house to socializing out on the patio, and it was like I was someone else.

In the small dining room just inside the sliding glass door, almost in view of where they sat—I could see their legs stretched on the chairs—I took a small glass monkey off a shelf full of decorative objects, hesitated for a moment, and, with a flick of my wrist, broke its long, winding tail against the edge of the shelf. The tail broke cleanly. I walked to the guest bedroom and hid the bulk of the monkey in my suitcase.

If I witnessed some kid do this now, I would say they were seeking attention, that it was a cry for help, a response to their mother getting hauled home by the cops. Or that they were going through a phase. But I have never stolen or purposely destroyed anything else my entire life, and I had no desire to be caught, and felt no catharsis or whatever one is supposed to feel after crying for help. More than anything, in retrospect, the act seemed to mark an accomplishment, like the medal one receives for finishing a marathon. By realizing that being alone and uncared for could be liberating, I earned the satisfaction that came along with breaking the tail off my aunt's monkey.

After I hid the evidence, I returned to the front room, with all its pictures of foreign places, and had an urge to throw a different knick-knack—a small ivory model of the Taj Mahal—through the front window. No, not an urge. I simply picked up the trinket and knew how breaking that window would make me feel. Just then, Denise called to me urgently. I assumed she was irritated by my prolonged absence, so I hurried outside.

Elaine was standing on the concrete with her hands on her hips. Her chair was folded flat on the ground next to her. Denise sat sideways on her own chair with her knees pointed away from Elaine. I had no idea what had happened, and for no good reason thought it was my fault.

"Here she is!" Elaine said when I came out. "And with no drinks!"

Cursing myself, I turned to go back in, but Elaine snagged a finger in my waistband to hold me up. Her bony knuckle poked my hip.

"I'll get them, honey," she said. "You set that chair up and sit. Don't want to get you dirty." She slipped out her finger, looked me up and down, patted the dirt from the seat of my shorts. "Boy, don't you look pretty in your outfit. Such a fashionable young lady. Doesn't she look good, Denise?"

Denise turned our way and nodded with little enthusiasm. Her lips were magenta from the wine cooler and her sunglasses a couple feet away in the grass. She looked tired, and older than she was. Uneasy concern quickly replaced any trace of the revelatory elation I had felt inside the house.

"Are you okay?" I whispered when we were alone. But Elaine was back before Denise could reply. I was selfishly relieved to not have to hear Denise's answer. I gave Elaine her seat back, and gladly took my place on the ground.

When they finished their drinks, Denise stood, stretched, and said she wanted to eat and get out of the sun, so we took Elaine's LeBaron to the Dairy Queen and ate burgers and shakes. Then we drove around town looking at the lake and the fancy lake homes. Elaine pointed out where the boat race was to take place the next day.

On the way home, Elaine pulled over, turned back to me, and said, "Come on up and take the wheel." I hoped Denise would spring to my aid, but she only smoked and stared out her window, which was barely cracked despite the oppressive heat. The smoke curled in the flat light of the setting sun. I'm still shocked that driving around in the swelter- ing, smoky car had not made me sick.

I hesitated, and Elaine hopped in the back seat next to me. Her knee touched mine and I was overwhelmed by her odor of smoke and beer, along with an acrid, chemical smell, like new shoes when you first open the box. Unnerved, I scurried into the driver's seat.

"You have to learn young," Elaine said, cracking a beer. "That's our way. Your dad chauffeured us around as soon as he could reach the pedals."

It's true, my dad made sure we all knew how to drive. He said that if he ever slumped over on the highway, we needed to be able to get him to the hospital. Mostly, though, my dad made my brothers drive our mother to work so he could have the car during the day.

As I inched onto the empty country road, I stuck my arm out the window to indicate I was merging. The turn signal in my parents' car had long been broken. Elaine laughed and said to bring my skinny arm back in before the wind snapped it in two. She reached ahead and clicked the lever to show me how it worked. Then, every so often as I drove, Denise reached over and corrected the position of the wheel. Elaine told me to step on it or we wouldn't make it back in time for *Night Court*.

We had forgotten to rent a movie and the only tape in Elaine's house was the Arnold Schwarzenegger movie *Raw Deal*, which she was late in returning, and which Denise refused to watch. Instead, we sat quietly through *Night Court* and the rest of the primetime lineup. I fell asleep during the local news and woke on the floor of the guest bedroom, sprawled on top of my sleeping bag, completely disoriented. I heard breathing on the nearby bed and began to panic when I could not find the opening of my sleeping bag.

"Which one are you?" I heard someone say.

My aunt stood in the doorway, her silhouette like a furry lollipop.

"I want to go home," I said.

"Not going to happen. She asleep?"

"I want to go home," I repeated.

"Come stay in my room if you're scared." She opened the door wider and stretched a hand toward me.

Denise's warning came to mind, and I scrambled around until I found the mouth of my bag and ducked inside. Light slivering in from the open door filtered through the polyester of the sleeping bag and made me feel as though I was in a rose-colored cocoon. I heard, "This family," and the click of the door.

## 5

I woke early, still in my clothes, and with no residual fear from the previous night. I quietly undressed and dressed so I did not disturb Denise. Elaine's snores were audible through the wall.

Being alone again agreed with me, and I hoped they would sleep all day, at least until I noticed that Elaine had no cereal. I rummaged through the cupboards like a starving raccoon, but everything was bare except for dusty cans of green beans and pumpkin pie filling. My desire for breakfast was so strong that I searched out Elaine's keys and, until I realized I had no money, considered driving to the store for some Fruity Pebbles and milk.

Elaine woke first and joined me on the patio. I had tried to eat the orange in her refrigerator, but it was inedible, so I threw it at the golf course, and there it sat, a few feet away, half-peeled, like a baseball with its cover hit off.

A different Elaine from yesterday, with her face scrubbed clean, eyes bloodshot. She smiled politely before easing herself into the chair next to mine. For a while we listened to the grasshoppers and locusts. There weren't any golfers.

"What time is it?" she asked.

"I don't know," I said.

"No golfers," she said.

I turned and looked at the course, as though to confirm it.

"Nice to wake up and not be alone," she said. "If I came out here, nice day like this, and it was empty out there, I'd probably bawl my eyes out."

This didn't move me back then. I had not yet known true loneliness and so was gratified that she was often unhappy. I was hungry and bored and hoped she would weep right then as punishment for ruining my vacation.

Eventually Elaine remembered the boat race. I had also forgotten and was immediately sure that we had missed all the best crashes. Frustration caused an acidic burn in the pit of my empty stomach. I blamed Denise for sleeping so late, having already grasped that Elaine was not to be counted on for practicalities. As the youngest child in a large family, I was used to being ignored, but could also expect a reasonable amount of care. Now I felt betrayed by the lack of consideration. I was forced to confront the fact that I was powerless to provide for myself.

## 6

She parked by a retaining wall that marked the end of a dead-end road, just in front of a sign that read No Outlet. Nothing like the marina I'd imagined. No bunting or banners, no kids up on their fathers' shoulders getting a better view of the powerboats.

We pushed through a small opening in a fence and entered an abandoned park. Wooden squares with pegs in the middle for playing horseshoes, a rotting picnic table, rusted monkey bars, all overgrown with grass. It was shady under the canopy of trees and there was no sign of water.

As Elaine walked ahead, toward a path carved into the adjoining woods, I instinctively stopped, preferring to stay in the park, even if it meant missing the race. To buy time, I stooped to tie my shoe, forgetting they were Velcro. I undid and redid them, staying down on one knee in the dirt.

Nearby, at the edge of the clearing, I saw a heap of fur, and a face. Shifting focus, I saw another. Surprisingly, I was not afraid at the sight of these long-dead animals. Instead, my frustration and hunger and disorientation seemed to disappear, or rather to transform into an intense but momentary sadness that these animals were left here all alone to rot.

Elaine came back.

"Two dead dogs," I said.

"Coyotes," she said.

We looked at them.

"They eat cats. People shoot them," she said.

She turned and left. To get away from the dead coyotes, I followed.

We made our way down the path until I heard the slap of water and distant shrieks and chatter of people. No roar of boat motors though. Elaine parted some bushes and the water opened in front of us. It was blue and sunny. A small outcropping of rocks jutted into the lake. Locals sat on a dock about thirty feet away. Relief flooded me. I tried to figure out why I'd been so worried ever since we left the car. We sat on separate rocks.

"Can't stand the crowds," Elaine said.

I nodded. There were white sails, all crowded together, across the lake.

"When does the race start?" I asked.

She lifted her eyebrows and pointed across the water at the sails.

"There's your race," she said.

"That's it?"

"Yep."

I laughed at myself, too thankful to be out of the creepy park to be angry. Of course it wasn't a powerboat race. This was a midsized lake in Wisconsin, not Lake Tahoe. I was proud of myself for never saying out loud how badly I wanted to watch the speedboats. If I couldn't see boats crash, I might as well have not appeared foolish.

We watched for a few minutes. The boats barely seemed to move. Once a sail tipped low, almost to the water, but it popped right back up. Even if it had capsized, though, it wouldn't have been as cool as those powerboats flopping and splintering at breakneck speed.

"Should we go?" I asked. "I'm hungry."

"Sure," she said. "I never understood what the big deal was about this race anyway."

7

Denise grabbed my arm and yanked me into the bedroom as soon as I stepped through the door. She shook my shoulders, told me to wake her up next time. She locked my eyes as though searching them for truth. Apparently satisfied with what she found, she repeated her earlier warning, but gently since I was already so confused and frightened by her reaction. I wondered what I had done wrong.

That evening Elaine and Denise drank more than the night before. They were slurring and boisterous by the time *Cheers* came on. I had a blast because the uncertain, even tumultuous mood since we arrived had finally settled, and they indulged me as if I were an entertaining dog. Being humored meant that I could perform for an audience, and so I delivered all my best material. I told Denise about the dead coyotes and made a show of how boring I found the boat race. I told them about this girl I hated, Jenny Feltz, who farted during math class, and everyone began calling her Jenny Farts, so she started skipping school and the teacher lectured us about name calling, and then everyone—even the teacher—lost it when one of the boys made his armpit fart during the teacher's speech. I told them a joke about two of our teachers—

named Mr. Peas and Mrs. Eckley—who were supposedly having an affair: *How do you know Mrs. Eckley is a vegetarian? Because she only eats Peas!* I began to sing a song from our end-of-the-year recital when Elaine interrupted. She said she hadn't eaten all day and wanted ice cream.

She tossed me her keys and said, "You're up."

I was not afraid but still appealed to Denise.

"I did when I was your age," she said.

Intoxicated by attention and confidence, I got behind the wheel and fired up the engine. Elaine joined Denise in the back seat and said to me, "A true chauffeur!"

As I drove, they provided me with helpful tips and compliments, and when the road we were traveling on terminated into a three-way junction, Elaine said to turn right, though the way I remembered it, the ice cream place was left.

"Back roads," she said. "Shortcut."

Now deeper into the farmland, with knee-high corn or scrubby soybeans on each side, an uncanny silence filled the car. I turned to see what was happening in the back.

"Eyes on the road, honey," Elaine said before I was able to get a look.

Every so often I heard hesitant murmurs coming from behind me. But I obeyed Elaine's instruction and concentrated on driving, suspecting that I was on my own to keep us going. Something—a foot perhaps— grazed my head but there was no apology, only a muffled sort of shriek. Soon a hand appeared and switched on the radio, which was tuned to an oldies station.

After that, the car was filled with 1950s pop music and an excess of stimulation, which I later believed was a sort of electricity created by the exploitation of ignorance and trust. It was thrilling and, in the moment, far from unpleasant. I held faith in them and did not recognize the extent of how wrong it all was. I merely focused on the section of road directly illuminated by the headlights, oversteered, and jerked the car around. But even as I prayed that no cars would come toward us, I enjoyed being behind the wheel. I was both in control and powerless. I was useful. I began to think my own thoughts and listen to the radio. Occasional panting or whispering came from the back seat, and it seemed as though I was a vital part of a real adult secret. Scary as it was, and though it has since haunted me, at the time it all felt normal, familial, and in retrospect I believe I acted admirably under the circumstances.

Ahead of us, six green dots gleamed on the side of the road. Three deer transfixed by the headlights. Reminded that there were dangers present beyond my shaky driving ability, I suddenly needed to know when this ride would end.

"Are we still going for ice cream?" I shouted over the radio.

When I didn't receive an answer, I glanced back and saw tangled feet and Elaine's dry, tan hand clenching the flesh of a leg. I swung my head straight, momentarily forgot the road, and jolted the car into a gentle fishtail. Before I could apologize for the disturbance, Denise grunted and screamed, "Get off get off get *off*!"

The rest happened quickly. The interior light flashed on, and I saw Elaine, whom Denise had apparently shoved, attempt to brace herself against the seat as the back door began to swing open. It only took a couple seconds, but in my memory, she hung in the open doorway for a long time, suspended, illuminated before the darkness of the fields and the night sky, hair tossed by the onrush, unzipped track jacket flapping, bra dangling below her pale breasts, with bugged eyes fastened on mine, and a ghostly moan coming from her mouth.

I neglected my duties and allowed the car to veer. We dipped down a shallow ditch between the road and a soybean field, the back door crashed against the ground and propelled Elaine back inside. Denise screamed, "Brake!" I panicked and blindly stomped my foot down on the gas pedal, rocketing us up the far side of the ditch. The car left the ground for a timeless second, during which I closed my eyes and hugged myself. We landed and I stabbed my foot down again, this time on the brake. We ground to a halt amongst the soybeans.

An Elvis song played. Rows of plants were lit by the headlights. The turn signal had been jostled on and every click bathed the soy to the right of us in yellow. Elaine and Denise continued to grasp each other for safety in the wake of the crash.

We exited the car. Elaine surveyed the damage with a hand over her mouth, Denise buttoned her pants, and I trembled.

"Well, that sure was something," Elaine said.

She walked around to inspect the door that had come open during their struggle, and which now hung like a disjointed limb. "Are you kids okay?" she finally asked. She focused on me and said, "Your mother's going to kill me."

"I won't tell," I said automatically.

Elaine sighed, nodded, and made her way toward the road. We silently followed, leaving the car in the field. Her house was not far away. Apparently, I had driven us in a big circle.

### 8

The last image I hold from that night, before I drifted off to sleep on the floor, is of Denise perched on the edge of the bed, wine cooler in hand, staring into the dark. In my mind she was watching over me. I have never been sure if she came along to keep me safe or if it just turned out that way, and though I would prefer it not to have happened, since it did, I choose to believe that I was witness to and benefitted from such a display of bravery.

The next morning, Denise took me home, two days early. When she parked in front of my house, she rested her forehead against the steering wheel and spoke for the first time since we got in the car. She said, "God. My life."

I put a hand on her shoulder and felt panic in my chest.

She looked over at me, her head still touching the wheel. She was tired. I know now that I wanted to say, "Did you come to protect me?" I wish I had said this, to let her know that I recognized she had done a good thing, whether she intended to or not. Saying it might have saved her like she saved me. Instead, I said, "People will wonder what's going on."

She sat up straight and nodded.

My mom deflated when she came home from work that afternoon and saw me in the living room. She tried not to sigh, I think, but she could not help it. I don't blame her though.

As if by instinct, I excitedly rattled off details about the trip—Dairy Queen, the golf course, the boat race. Apparently, Aunt Elaine had called my mom at work and explained that she was not feeling well and so had sent us home. I blinked a couple times when my mom told me this and said, "Yeah. She threw up."

My mom made a face and went into the kitchen to start dinner. I felt a bit queasy and anxious to talk. I went around and opened bedroom doors and checked the backyard, even the bathroom, but everyone was out. I did not dare go down to the basement to see my dad. In my room, which I shared with Linda, I took out the little broken-tailed glass monkey I had stolen from my aunt and placed it on a shelf next to seashells and pretty rocks and prize ribbons and framed pictures of me and my friends. I became momentarily infused by the pleasant sensation of being alone in my aunt's living room.

Denise never finished college. That spring she quit school and ran off with a married attorney. They lived in Arizona for a while before he went back to his family. She never came back, though, and kept herself out of touch. I heard different things over the next few years—mostly through overheard jokes or derisive comments made by my snarky relatives. That she lived in a commune in Colorado. That she worked as a hostess at a casino. I can't bring myself to guess what role damage played in her choices, just as I rarely speculate what role chance and atmospheric conditions have played in my own life. And while the general view of my siblings—especially my brothers—is that she's a failure and a lost cause, I can't help but feel something like envy when I imagine all Denise has experienced since she escaped our family orbit.

As for me, that day, I sat on my bed and gazed at my monkey until I heard the front door open, and slam closed. Soon the door opened and closed again, and then again. I heard voices outside—my brother Bobby had a friend over, my brother Steve complained to my mom about what she was making for dinner. My dad came up from the basement. They were all home, just outside my room, and I stayed in there, alone, for one extra minute. For a minute I sat and stared at my monkey, and then I left my room to join them.

# Résumé

At a recent job interview I was told to give an example of how I failed during previous employment and what I learned from that experience. It was not a question. The interviewer implied that I have had a regenerative outcome following failure; indeed, she must have assumed that everyone she will ever interview has flopped in some inspirational way that has molded them into the ideal job seeker they are today.

I stifled an urge to say, "Maybe I'm an unqualified success and have learned nothing!"

But I suppose they figure that if the applicant had never failed, they would not be applying for the jobs I am seeking, especially at my age. I played ball. I told a story about a time I forgot my gimbal at a shoot for a low-budget commercial and had to improvise with this other clamp that I always carry with me in case of an emergency. I learned the value of preparation, how to keep a cool head, and so on. That never happened, of course. I had anticipated the question and concocted the gimbal story the night before. I told that and many other lies to this HR representative who was to decide if I were to become a cameraman for the local ABC network affiliate.

On the drive home from the botched interview, I lambasted myself for giving inane answers to her unsurprising questions as well as for my lengthy pauses and lost trains of thought. A humiliating commute of shame. I slunk away with my tail between my legs and the taste of defeat menacing my tongue. Sensing a spiral, I attempted to cheer myself up by thinking of honest stories I could have told my interviewer about past growth-producing professional failures. It's my style to replace the prospect of solace with the surety of jokes at my own expense.

~

When he was fifteen and I was ten, my brother and I received Ken Norton boxing gloves for Christmas at his request. Back then I was the tallest, thinnest kid in my class, and he was two years away from being a First-Team All-Southern Lakes Conference linebacker. And though he was never a particularly caring brother, he was never violent either, until we got these gloves. That thin layer of polyester stuffing apparently protected him from having to face up to his brutality. These boxing matches were also the longest stretches of time we have ever spent alone together without watching TV. They were the only times he invited me into his room.

While we boxed there were two rules: he could not hit me in the head, and I could not cry out loud enough for our mom to hear. If he did punch me in the face then, by rule, I would have a free shot at his face with both his arms behind his back. If I yelped too loud, he could punch my face for the rest of the round. His gloves slipped to my jaw plenty of times, but I never dared take full advantage of my free shot, for fear of repercussion, so these rules were more to his benefit than mine.

I came up with a system: since I only had to protect myself from my waist to my neck, I crossed my arms in an X across my chest and abdomen and absorbed the blows. I never threw a punch. The bouts became an exercise in how many punches I could take, which I was fine because I got to spend time in my brother's room. I don't know what he got out of it. Someone to punch, I guess.

I developed a deep bruise in the direct center of my bony forearms, at the spot where they crossed. The bruise eventually turned yellow, then a bright green, so even my fourth-grade teacher, who years before had boxed Golden Gloves, took an interest in it. For about a week, before my teacher forgot about it, I was a minor celebrity in my school because each day began with me standing in front of the class to show how the bruise widened and changed colors like a mood ring.

I nearly put an end to the boxing when my brother either realized that according to our rules rabbit punches were almost legal or he got tired of punching my crossed forearms. Whatever the reason, one evening he punched me hard in the shoulder so that I spun around, and then he haymakered me in the kidney.

He knelt beside me while I gasped on the carpet. Bafflingly, I was touched by his concern. He told me that I was a tough guy, and tough guys stand up. He tried tough love. He asked, "You think Ali would stay down this long? You think Ali'd cry like that?" He used to say that he was Rocky Marciano, and I was Muhammad Ali. Thinking back on it, that's pretty racist. My brother surely chose Marciano because he was the only decent White boxer that came to mind.

When I regained the ability to move, he barred the door until I promised not to squeal. In exchange I was given permission to deliver two free shots to his face. I took them wholeheartedly and was disappointed at the result. I told him to hand over his gloves so I could throw them away. He did not agree to those terms, and his willingness to bargain softened my resolve. We made a deal that, going forward, he would pay me a quarter for every round I boxed. This was my first paying job.

All spring I was his punching bag. Soon enough I lost all feeling in my forearms, so the toughest part was hiding the bruise from my mom. The bruise was beautiful. It turned from green to purple to magenta and settled on a kind of sunset of oranges and reds. The kids at school were aware of my contractual agreement and gazed at the bruise with a kind of fearful respect. They would ask, in awed tones, how much my earnings were up to. I always said I didn't know, though I kept a strict tally in a notebook hidden under my mattress.

The paid rounds began in May. By July the total was over thirty dollars.

My brother eyed me suspiciously when I requested payment. I said, as though for clarification, that I wanted to buy a basketball. He laughed.

When he saw I was serious, his face settled into a pragmatic expression that I had never seen on him before. It was as though a researcher had been playing chess with a monkey for months and was caught off guard by a check. He said I couldn't possibly expect him to pay, right? He had no recollection of any deal and seemed to genuinely suspect that I was trying to put one over on him.

I did something then that I was always proud of: I didn't cry, or stomp, or threaten to squeal to mom. I boxed a normal round, and when the moment was right, I dropped to a knee and gave him one to the nuts as hard as I could. I had boxed one hundred and thirty-two rounds without throwing a punch. He never saw it coming. While he writhed on the carpet, I pried the gloves off his hands, ran outside, climbed to the top of our tallest tree, and knotted both sets of gloves to the top limb—as far as I know they are still up there, dangling like sneakers from a power line. I lingered in that tree, enjoying the relative safety. I rubbed my arms, watched the sun set, and surveyed for danger. I sat up there into the night, until my mother's threats turned tearful.

≈

At thirteen, I was the youngest employee at the Piggly Wiggly, and because of this the other stockers ragged on me. Their favorite joke was to say that I was only hired because my mom slept with the owner, whose name was Glen. They didn't intend to hurt my feelings—such jokes were commonly exchanged—but it did get me thinking. I hadn't applied; one day at the start of summer vacation as I sat in my underwear watching *The Price Is Right*, my mom simply informed me that I was to report to the grocery store the next day wearing black pants. It was also true that my dad wasn't home much that summer and that Glen went easier on me than the rest of the guys on the stock crew.

Stocking groceries is tedious, and once, when conversation waned, one of the guys asked me if I ever caught my mom doing it with Glen. I said that indeed I had. They perked up. They asked for details and so

I spun a tale of sexual goings-on about Glen and my mom doing it on a pool table. Basically, I summarized a *Penthouse Forum* story I'd read about a million times during my frequent perusals through the stack of dirty magazines my brother kept in his bottom desk drawer.

It didn't take long for these stories to become a common way to pass the time. When I ran out of material, I asked my brother to buy me my own *Penthouse Forum* magazine (which he did after extracting an exorbitant fee) and each night before work I memorized a new scenario for my mom and Glen to get into. I remember one took place at a cabin, where both my mom and dad and Glen and his wife were staying on vacation. In this scenario, my dad and Glen's wife left to get more wine and while they were gone, my mom and Glen ass-fucked so much that they had to shower off. When their spouses came back and asked about their wet hair, Glen said coolly, "Well, Dave, I just ass-fucked your wife so hard that we had to shower off," and my dad only laughed, thinking Glen would never say that if it had actually happened. Later, I realized at least one of these guys I worked with had probably jerked off to the thought of my mother and Glen. I'm sure I would have if I were in their position. I certainly did while memorizing the scenarios.

The guys on the overnight stock crew were ruthless, and so I always made sure to save the best stories for when I closed, since our shifts overlapped. Once, I told a real doozy about my mom and Glen at a rodeo. While the overnight guys were gathered in the break room, I told them how my mom was a bucking bronco. I wasn't supposed to be on break, and one of the guys had given me a cigarette—which I pretended to smoke—and just as I finished my performance, I saw their eyes collectively shift to the doorway, where, I discovered, Glen had been listening to my story about him wearing only a cowboy hat, fucking my mother, who was clad only in chaps, in the dirt under the rodeo bleachers.

I put my half-finished cigarette behind my back and bit my lip. Glen told me that he wasn't an idiot; he could see the smoke rising behind me. Then he made me repeat the whole story, which I did, while the overnight guys put their fists to their mouths to stifle their laughter. Glen called my mom in and made me repeat the entire rodeo story yet again, in front of them both. I was fired, and that weekend my mom made me repeat the story over and over to my dad while I smoked an entire pack of cigarettes.

My poor dad, I think now. It was as much a punishment for him as it was for me. The whole thing was my mom's idea. My dad watched sheepishly as I hacked and sobbed and described how my own mother—his wife—was fucked by another man at a rodeo. She probably imposed this sentence on purpose, to admonish my dad for being away from home so much. That's how my mom operated. Out on the road as often as my dad was, I'm sure he thought about my mom with other guys. My father worked hard, and I highly doubt my mom ever cheated on him, but I'll bet the next time he went out he worried about it even more. He didn't want to hear me say those awful things. Stories like that are for break rooms.

~

The summer after I graduated high school, I gamed it to where I could work these two jobs on a double shift for a year and then take two years off to figure things out. The plan was to make a bundle and, not able to spend it anyway since I was always on the job, I'd save twice as much. I worked third shift on the line at Generac, a factory where we made some automobile part—something to do with the seat-adjustment mechanism in GM cars—and during the day I drove a forklift at the warehouse of a Walmart. Somewhere along the line I had picked up the idea that freedom was the most a person could strive for, and that the only good reason to work was to pay for time. Not that I don't agree with this now. Only now I wonder what to do with the time I have. I try to figure out why time is important. I fail to definitively define the meaning of balance.

Back then I didn't overthink it. Time was a carrot to work toward, five days a week, sixteen hours a day, plus an hour driving, with five hours sleep in between. I'd go out to my car and smoke half a joint during each of my four breaks and both lunches. Weekends I'd sleep. The whole time, sleep.

By September I had lost most of my friends to college, or else we weren't close enough to make an extra effort. The people at work were just there, hovering around me like figures in a dream. All that time was like a dream, since I spent equal time at warehouse, factory, and sleep. It's shocking how much sense the world makes when it is so evenly apportioned. In retrospect, this was the most satisfying era of my life, though I would never willingly do it again. Both jobs required concentration, not thought, and outside of work I was too tired to worry. If I'd had only one shift per day, I would have spent the rest of my time wondering what I should do, why I was doing what I was doing, and if I should chuck it all for something greater.

My plan ended abruptly. My grandmother died. Not unexpectedly, exactly, and I decided that sticking to my plan was more important than attending the funeral. I did not miss a shift. However, the introduction of death into my thoughts—indeed, the comparison and weighing of death and work—made the air of the factory heavy, the sounds of machinery grating, the boxes coming off trucks never-ending. It made my fingers, which had become instruments for the connection of tiny parts, as dexterous as loaves of bread. I lost all the fluidity I had spent months honing. In short, I began to think.

I had just gotten to be one of those guys who could gun the forklift, with full load, backward straight away from the truck, get it turned in the opposite direction, and speed away without shifting a single box. After I skipped that funeral to instead keep on working toward some vague notion of carrot time, I tried to keep straight. I stopped smoking pot. I was cautious. At Generac my parts per hour dropped. At Walmart I dumped entire loads. The other guys started to resent me for clogging the system.

My mom forgave me for skipping the funeral. Her forgiveness changed nothing. The spell was broken. At Walmart I dropped a pallet of glassware. My second in a week. I can still picture how it tipped, slowly, from the top, until it fell almost completely upside down. The plastic shrink wrap held it in place. The glass scattered across the concrete floor in all four directions equally. A shard cut the receiving clerk's ankle.

I was fired, and that night, at Generac, I was fired again. For what I don't remember. I was so tired. Point is that now, when I recall this time of my life, I don't think about the money I made, or how I was able to loaf for the next four months. What comes to mind is when I walked onto the factory or warehouse floor at the start of my shift. How I'd look at the machines and trucks and forklifts and recognize how impressive it all was. I took pride in my ability to wield such imposing equipment. I was aware of my capabilities. I had adapted to the intricacies of a system.

~

A couple years later, on the county road crew, I drove around in an orange truck with the windows rolled down. Every day was incredibly hot. We filled in potholes and loaded bloated deer in the bed of the truck, flung raccoon carcasses deep into the woods with our shovels. The guy I worked with was twenty years older than I was and barely said a word to me. He'd just stop the truck and nod backward and I'd wake up, walk back, and figure out if something needed to be filled, loaded, or flung. In the heat of the day, we would stop at a creek, and he'd fish. Anything he caught he would slap against the rocks and toss back in, not considering if he had done enough to kill it.

Once a week we cleaned the park bathrooms. Or I would while he smoked in the truck or at a picnic table. A couple months after I started, we were in Elmhurst Park, out near the fairgrounds, and I carried the rolls of toilet paper, plastic bags, paper-dispenser keys, broom, paper towels, and air freshener into the bathroom, and promptly dropped them as I saw that a man had shot himself, with a shotgun. Only his legs, and the non-barrel end of the gun, were poking out from one of the stalls. Directly in front of the stall opening, "IF THESE" was written in green marker on the wall, but the thought was not finished. I wanted to ask the coroner, later, if the man had a marker on him, but it didn't seem appropriate.

Outside, I stood next to the open window of the truck. Out of habit my hands went for my pockets, and I realized how badly they were shaking. He did not notice me as he smoked and stared straight ahead, though I was six inches away. Finally, I said, "Willy," and he gave a start, looked frightened for a moment, and followed me to the bathroom, where I pointed inside. He was in there for no more than a few seconds, came out, lit a cigarette, then looked at me and said, "Third one." I later learned that this was not an entirely unusual event. When he finished his cigarette, he walked to the truck and radioed it in, and we sat at a picnic table and waited.

Outside of funerals and hospitals, I've seen six dead bodies in my life. I believe this to be a high number. Once I drove by a car accident just as it happened and saw a woman crushed in her seat. My friend Brian Wilkes fell dead of a heart attack during a league game at a bowling alley. Twice I walked by and saw old folks peacefully dead: one on a porch and one at a bus stop. And in my first season of varsity baseball, I went in to talk to my coach and he just sat there at his desk, cold. I spoke to him for five minutes, worried that his silence meant he was taking me out of the rotation.

Whether I have been lucky, unlucky, or am just more observant than most people I don't know. But this one at the park has stuck with me. It is the only one that comes to me when I wish it wouldn't.

We only stopped working long enough to allow two police cruisers and an ambulance to arrive, and I gave a statement to the police. At the next park we ate lunch at the tables, I at one and Willy at the other because his family joined him each week when we cleaned the park bathrooms. They talked and laughed. I am not sure if Willy mentioned anything to them. Willy used to kiss his son goodbye on the lips, though his son was too old for this. His son was a fat boy who used to snort. He probably still lives around here.

That afternoon we went fishing as usual. When Willy caught a bass, he unhooked it and gripped it by the tail, raised it up. Somewhere I found it within myself to speak and said, "Willy, don't," and he stopped.

He looked up at it, then at the water, shrugged, and tossed it to me. I caught it with a snap of my wrist—pushing it away rather than gathering it into myself, like snagging a lazy line drive—and placed it in the water.

I realize I have never told this story before. Yes, the part about the dead man, many times, but not the part about the fish. I look back on this with pride. It was a situation I believe myself to have properly handled.

# Vultures

After snows, Paul had to drive up to Denali to plow. He would drive an hour and a half up there and plow out the parking lot and driveway in case any visitors were stuck in the rental cabins. This time, it had snowed about eight inches overnight into the morning, and he left for Denali around noon, after the snow had stopped and the highway had been cleared. He worked maintenance for the Susitna district of Alaska State Parks, which covered all state property from Willow to Denali, and plowing was his favorite part of the job, even though on this trip he had a hemorrhoid and sitting for so long in the truck irritated it terribly.

He stopped to get gas and cigarettes and apply balm. Then he sat in his parked truck and slowly unwrapped his Mavericks as he enjoyed the relief. That's when a woman appeared at his window and asked for a ride. He had seen her hanging around the register when he bought the cigarettes and had not given her much thought. But it was cold out and Paul liked company, so he tilted his head toward the passenger seat. As she opened the door, he stifled a grin. That he received a thrill from such intimate proximity to a woman who was not his wife, as well as from subverting state park regulations, proved to Paul how dull his life had become.

She got in and said thanks, and Paul nodded and consciously did not look at her as he pulled out onto the highway. He had not thought to ask why she was hanging out at the Tesoro station or where she was ultimately headed until after she was already in, and by then he figured that the particulars did not matter. The electric lighter popped, and Paul extracted it with a shaking hand and lit a cigarette. He was not scared, his hands just trembled almost all the time now. Most likely nerves. He had never brought up the affliction with his doctor because the quiver subsided whenever he was required to perform an intricate task.

The woman had on a navy-blue snowsuit. A green-and-white stocking cap.

"Figured someone would let me in," she said.

Paul pushed down his eyebrows, glanced in her direction without moving his head.

"Someone did," Paul said.

She laughed, took off her cap. Paul wanted to see what her hair did with the cap off, but instead he took his hands off the wheel of the truck, tipped the ash of his cigarette into his palm, and smeared the ashes into the pocket of his coveralls. They were not supposed to smoke in the truck.

The woman grabbed the wheel when Paul did this, though there was no need. Her hand moved automatically, like this gesture was part of their routine. Paul was fine with the informality, despite his sense that it was an attempt to gain trust.

They drove past Paul's favorite spot on this route. A bunch of white birch on both sides of the highway had been cut away so there was about thirty yards of stumps in both directions for a half-mile stretch of road. Chopped down to prevent a wildfire from jumping the highway. He often imagined the excitement of driving along with fires raging on each side of him, knowing he was safe. In the summer, Paul thought it looked like a bed of nails, because the stumps were so thin. He told this to her.

"Bed of nails?" the hitcher said. "Can't see it. The hell knows though, covered in snow. Covered like it is looks more like gravestones."

Paul nodded. They did look like gravestones.

"I'd offer you a cigarette, but we can't smoke in here," Paul said. He pinched the lit end of his cigarette between his fingers, placed the butt in his coveralls, and zipped the pocket. "I do, but I'm not supposed to."

"My brother-in-law, ex-brother-in-law, my sister's old husband, smoked those e-cigarettes. Lots of people do, I guess," she said. "Say, you mind taking me up to Talkeetna?"

Paul looked at her directly for the first time. Her hair was short and wispy and sticking out in tufts from how she pulled off the hat. She was older than Paul, maybe midforties. Bags under her eyes. A tough chin and red, crooked nose.

"The hell you mean? Talkeetna's a half hour out of my way, one way." He was going to keep on, but his voice began to rise in pitch, like it did when he fought with his wife. There was no reason to argue when he was only doing her a favor, and getting riled only made him seem afraid, so he stopped talking. Still, he felt the dissatisfaction of having lost an argument.

The hitcher put her hands by the heat vents and did not say anything. A moose was on the side of the road, waiting to pass over the highway.

"Moose," Paul said.

"You pay for the gas in this thing?" she asked.

"They give me a gas card," Paul said proudly.

"Anybody back where you came from watching the clock, waiting for you to get back on time?"

"South of Willow." After he said it, Paul realized she had not asked where he was coming from. "No, they ain't watching the clock. I'm taking the truck home with me tonight."

Paul knew she was only trying to talk him into taking her to Talkeetna. "I'm not taking you," he said. "I can't."

"It's a long trip walking," was all she said. "Cold out there."

Paul thought of his reply—which would have been: *Then you should have stipulated where you needed to go before you got in*—but figured he would get all flustered and high-pitched while speaking, so it was better to let the matter rest.

The turn for Talkeetna was fifteen minutes ahead and Paul wanted another cigarette but didn't want to offer one to her. The desire, combined with the bug-bite itch of his hemorrhoid stirring back to life, made him squirm.

Of course, they might have expected him to come back to the office—Paul was not entirely sure. There was time to finish plowing and be back before the office closed if he hurried. But he had the authority to take the truck home, that was fact. Only he, Mike, and the ranger worked fulltime at the district office anyway, so if he did not return in time those two would, at worst, goad him, claim he was shirking—Mike and the ranger enjoyed banding together against Paul whenever possible. They were both nearing retirement, had worked together their whole lives, and still considered Paul new. The two of them had all kinds of inside jokes that Paul made a show of not caring to be in on, and so they gleefully kept him ignorant, as they were fully aware how much being left out bothered him. Paul had only been there three years, and was the youngest by over twenty years, but he knew more about machines than the other two put together. They were more knowledgeable about district operations, sure, but Paul would learn that too, over time. What this push and pull of knowledge versus experience mostly boiled down to was that when Paul fixed something the other two were unable to figure out, and rejoiced in his ability, they were still able to get a rise out of him, lately by referencing his hemorrhoid—which he had unwisely mentioned a while back. Most of the time they all got along though. Paul liked his job. They just liked to push Paul's buttons more than he liked them pushed. Which was why they liked to push them so much.

Like how they pranked him. Their favorite was to exploit his ophidiophobia by throwing a rubber hose or a broken snow machine belt at him and yelling, "Snake!" After falling for it for a few months, Paul stopped flinching and grabbed the hose or belt out of the air, until Mike tossed him a live garter snake that he had purchased at a pet store in Anchorage. Ever since then Paul had no choice but to curse and scamper whenever a serpentine object was lobbed in his direction.

"Know what I did today?" Paul asked.

"What?"

"Just before I took off, I removed all the bolts in their desk chairs so when they sit down, they'll fall right over."

She laughed and said, "Who?"

Paul looked annoyed. "Wilber and Mike."

She chuckled. "That's a good one. Know a guy who threw out his back after someone did that to him. Couldn't get off the couch for a week. Hilarious."

Heat jolted him. Paul had removed the bolts in his coworkers' chairs in retaliation for them placing a lifelike snake in his top desk drawer. Wilber, the ranger, had bought the toy snake during a trip to Arizona and mailed it to Paul, who fell off his own chair when he opened the box. Ever since then the snake has popped up from time to time. Paul wished he had cut the thing into pieces when he first opened the package, because now Wilber claimed that he spent good money on that snake and that Paul had no right to destroy it.

But the chair prank. Wilber, who was Paul's boss, had a bad back. He always wore a brace over his ranger uniform that Paul and Mike mocked surreptitiously.

Paul took out his cigarettes and offered one to the hitcher. She took it. When the lighter popped out, she lit up, and didn't roll down her window.

"Not that I don't want to take you," Paul said, speaking through pursed lips as he tried to light his cigarette on the cooling lighter. "Just that if anyone sees me, you know, someone I work with or someone from a different district . . ." He couldn't gather his thoughts. The lighter was not lighting his cigarette. A small ball of fire was being stoked underneath him. He writhed violently in his seat, jammed the lighter back into the slot, and blurted, "I can't just go wherever I want to go."

"I get it." She slumped down and flicked ash onto the floor mat. "Just that you're a nice guy, and you never know who'll pick you up out here. Thought maybe I could even buy you a beer when we get up there. To thank you."

The turn off for Talkeetna was in five miles. He lit his cigarette. He shifted his weight to spread his cheeks apart. The fact was that he was afraid of breaking a rule, though he did not consider himself to be a man who put such stock in regulations. He also looked forward to plowing. But turning down her request would add another irritation—the lost opportunity would aggravate him worse than his hemorrhoid—and he would be unable to enjoy the simple pleasure of a job completed. Other parks workers did worse: folks in other districts bragged about smoking pot in the truck, using their trucks to move house, or taking the truck down to strip clubs in Anchorage. Maybe driving up to Talkeetna was not such a bad idea. The ramifications of the chair prank made him want to avoid the office. Sure, the hitcher was trying to sucker him, but she was in a bad spot and needed his help—it was too cold to drop her off at the side of the road. Also, it was difficult for Paul not to factor in that picking up a woman hitchhiker was a top-tier sexual fantasy for him, even if he had no immediate plans to cheat on his wife and he was not attracted to this particular woman, with her frozen cheeks and crooked nose. But she was a woman, and it's not like Paul considered himself such a catch. He added it up: wrong to abandon her out in the cold, probably nobody would find out, still plenty of time to finish plowing, and he could visualize the erotic potentialities of the scenario the next time he had sex with his wife. Paul sighed, placed a hand underneath himself, and wriggled. He would take her where she needed to go.

At the bar, the Settler's Inn, Paul sipped the beer the woman bought him. His reasons for making the trip now seemed unfounded and he wished he was on his way north to Denali. He took pleasure in plowing and was only able to do it a few times a year. Instead of savoring the cozy bar and a simple transgression, his mind was on his outside-in plowing system, working from the perimeter of the lot into the middle. Not the most efficient method, but worth it for the pattern that developed. The snow dropped away into reduced rectangles until all at once nothing remained.

The woman, Wendy, had not stopped talking since they arrived. Her stories smacked of lies, though Paul could not figure why she bothered, unless she was winding him up or putting one over on him, so he remained wary. She told him her brother worked picking bananas for Chiquita and that she had a boyfriend once who lit a child on fire as a joke. She left the table to make a call, and Paul only stayed put because otherwise he would always wonder how the interaction turned out. Yet another situation he found himself in where any decision made him miserable.

"You know this town was what they based that show *Northern Exposure* on?" Wendy asked when she sat back down. "You remember that show? Or you too young?"

"I'm thirty-six," Paul said. He remembered the show. Joel. Ed. That fat Indian.

"Know what my dad did?" she asked. "He was the caretaker at the cemetery over in Tok, where I grew up. Winters he'd go out there whenever anyone died, load them into a Conex trailer, because it was too cold to dig. When it warmed up, they'd take them out and bury them. Every day after the thaw there'd be two, three burials."

"I went to Wilber's mom's funeral like that last June. She died in January," Paul said.

She nodded, took a sip, and continued talking.

"Did it until he was seventy-five and died when his house collapsed in a storm. But this one time I was helping him with a burial, and we were there waiting for a service to finish, just sitting on the trailer where we kept the equipment, watching from behind the priest or reverend or whatever. Preacher. So, it gets over and my dad fires up the tractor and we go over there."

"Sounds about right," Paul said.

She nodded. "Took away the chairs and turf, lowered the casket, and I jump down on top of it, rock it back and forth while my dad shimmied out the straps from underneath."

"That's the job." Paul respected when she trod the firm ground of truthful expertise.

Wendy continued. "While I'm down there this lady with goddamn sequins in her black dress came up to my dad and called us both vultures."

"Vultures?"

"Goddamn vultures," she said, forthright in anger. "Because of how we were sitting there behind the preacher waiting for it to be over. I mean, I'm not more than fourteen years old. You do three burials a day and it's not like each one is so goddamn special."

"Vultures," Paul said.

"No worse creature than a vulture," she said. "You ever been called a vulture?"

Paul shook his head. He had though, a couple months ago. While he hovered outside Wilber's office, waiting to get his time sheet signed, Paul heard Wilber say over the phone, "Hold on one minute while I get rid of this vulture."

The bar radio was tuned to the local contemporary country station broadcast from a house just down the street. A Rascal Flatts song played. When Paul took his daughters to see Talkeetna two summers ago, while it was busy with climbers waiting to get flown out to the base of the mountain, Paul parked across from the radio station, and they all watched the DJ through a big glass window. Her mouth moved a couple seconds before they heard what she said on the car stereo. At least initially, his girls were thrilled by the DJ.

Now, here in the same town, this manageable indiscretion stimulated Paul in a way that he could not quantify. A niggling, not-totally-unpleasant sense of danger troubled and sharpened his thoughts, though there appeared to be little for him to lose.

"Where do you come from?" Wendy asked after a long silence.

"Wisconsin. Born and raised in a town called Prairie du Chien," Paul said. "Right on the Mississippi River. Moved up here about ten years ago. Needed a change in scenery. Got in the car and drove all the way in a straight shot."

"Is that where all those serial killers are from? Isn't that what Wisconsin's famous for?" She stubbed one of his cigarettes out into the ashtray.

"One thing, I guess," Paul said.

She smiled, but not like before, back when she lied to him—this was a real, almost sad smirk. "Let's say I'm being friendly. Can we say I'm friendly? Am I friendly?"

Paul nodded. Ever since the vulture conversation, he was okay with her.

"Just for laughs, let's say I made a suggestion." She raised her eyebrows.

"You're friendly." Paul was ready to take control. Circumstances, he believed, would soon be resolved.

Before she could continue, though, the door banged open, and a man walked in. When Wendy saw him, she barked out a laugh. "Cubby," she called, waving to get his attention.

Cubby was a big guy, round, with a white beard stained yellow around the mouth. It was not snowing, but he slapped his stocking hat against his leg as though to knock off flakes. With barely a nod to Paul, he sat next to Wendy and began talking as though they were already in the middle of a conversation. Paul tried to follow along, since Wendy had hooked him with her promise of a proposition, but she and Cubby had intimate knowledge. They referred to people Paul did not know and laughed hard at inside jokes that they did not bother to explain. Their rudeness agitated Paul. As he grinded his hemorrhoid against the hard wooden stool, he thought of the searing pain described by Civil War soldiers torn into by musket balls. His cigarettes were out on the table, but he did not smoke because he preferred not to offer one to Cubby. He coughed but they kept talking.

Without a word, Paul got up, went to the bathroom, and applied some Prep H. Calling it "Prep H" had become a joke between him and his wife. She bought the store brand. The joke had evolved over time. Soothed, by the time Paul washed his hands, he made up his mind to leave the bar without even a goodbye. All told, this side trip would have wasted about two hours of his day. Still time to plow. He would microwave a burrito at the BP and eat it on the drive.

Wendy and Cubby both perked up when Paul emerged from the bathroom.

"Say, that your rig out there? Parks truck?" Cubby asked Paul, with admiration.

"Biggest one we got. For the major jobs. Plow detaches," Paul said.

Cubby whistled.

"See, I told you," Wendy said to Cubby. She winked at Paul.

Paul sat down.

"You work down in Willow?" Cubby asked.

"Nearabouts," Paul said. "Nancy Lake. I'm one of three guys down there to take care of the entire recreation area, plus plow the whole Susitna district in winter. Park alone's almost twenty-three thousand acres."

Cubby leaned in close to Paul. "I ask you something?"

His breath smelled peppery, like beef stew.

Wendy smiled. "We're friends. Ask him anything."

Paul nodded and sipped the fresh beer in front of him.

"As friends," Cubby said, "if I said we could make some money together, would you be interested?"

"Money?" Paul asked.

"You need money. Everyone needs money," Wendy said to Paul.

"I got some," Paul said, a little confused. "Was able to buy a new Glock forty-five with what was left of the dividend." Not long ago every Alaskan had received their yearly twelve-hundred-dollar check from the state for letting the oil companies drill the land. The forty-five, along with two other handguns, were locked in cases in Paul's bedroom closet.

"Can always use more though," Cubby said.

Paul shrugged. He didn't think much about money when he had a job.

"You don't have to do anything," Cubby said. "We only need to use your truck. Couple, three, four hours. You stay here with Wendy. I can handle the work."

"My truck?"

"You know he'd bring it back," Wendy said, reaching over and covering Paul's hand with her own. "Can't steal a big truck like that. Decals and everything. They'd catch him quick. Nowhere to hide it."

Paul slipped his hand out from under hers. He was aware that he should bolt out the door. "What you need it for?"

"Five hundred dollars," Cubby said. "All you do is sit here with Wendy."

Paul took off his cap, wiped his head as though he were sweating, then remembered he had thus far worn the hat to cover his baldness. He put his cap back on.

"Is it legal?" Paul only asked to buy time.

A woman with two giant malamutes entered the bar. Cubby watched the trio with interest. Wendy nodded to the Big & Rich song on the radio.

Their silence annoyed Paul. They could at least let him in on it, considering they asked him to take the risk. He lit a cigarette with trembling hands and tossed the pack in front of him. Wendy took one. Cubby continued to stare at the woman and her dogs. Paul exhaled, laughed through his nose, and said, "Jesus." He was done with them.

Wendy shrugged. Cubby wiped his open hand across the table as though to say the slate was wiped clean.

Paul needed a minute. If he got in his truck and drove away, he would feel as though he were running from a fight. But he was mad, not scared. He did not examine the nature of his anger, but what was foremost in his mind was the waste of time.

Outside, he was struck by all the white. Such purity allowed him to recalibrate, and he gained clarity. Check his phone, a last dose of Prep H, look them both in the eye, say farewell, and head off. He had

landed himself in this ugly situation and would extricate himself as
well. He did not blame them. Those two and Paul just happened to be
at cross purposes. And despite not wanting any part of their scheme,
the request was not unprecedented. He read in the papers about a state
trooper who was arrested last year for delivering supplies to meth labs
hidden deep in the woods. Their hope was that a police vehicle would
be above suspicion.

Talkeetna was a quaint and quiet town outside of climbing season.
A main street with a few bars, a couple souvenir stores, an ice cream
shop, the radio station. Across the street from Paul was a town square,
whose main feature was an old horse-drawn carriage inside a glass-front
building. There was a plaque that probably explained about the carriage, and Paul noticed a man sitting in the snow below it with his back
propped against the glass, his head tilted down, and his legs splayed in
front of him. Paul would have made sure the poor guy was all right if
not for his own pressing problems. Just then the man's head snapped
up. Paul shivered, lit a cigarette, and turned on his phone.

One new message left a half hour earlier, from Mike, who apparently
had started speaking before the message began to record.

" . . . heading to the hospital. Wilber's hurt. Came back from plowing
up at the trailhead and Wilber was flat on his back in his office. Looks
bad. Where are you? Pick up your goddamn phone. His chair was broke.
You know anything about it? Mine was busted too. Yours was fine. Hope
to hell you didn't have anything to do with this. It's serious. They might
have to operate. Call back."

Paul slipped his phone back into his pocket. He took two steps in the
direction of his truck and froze. He tapped the keys in the pocket of
his coveralls. The man, he noticed, was no longer sitting in the snow,
indeed was nowhere to be seen. Paul felt short of breath and needed to
organize his thoughts. It dawned on him that he might be out of a job
by the time he got back to the office, and that it was his own fault.
Well, to be fair, Wilber set things off by putting the snake in Paul's desk
drawer, but, Paul conceded, it was likely impossible to explain such an

escalation. He went back in the bar, passed the meth dealers without a glance, and entered the bathroom, where he peeled down his coveralls and lowered his pants.

There was a knock on the door. "Paul, let me in a second." It was Wendy.

"Let me alone," he said. "You got me into enough trouble." Only then did he consider that it might be best to keep his options open if he were to be fired.

The metallic jangling of a lock being picked or otherwise unbolted followed. Decency overrode Paul's panic and he decided to cover rather than defend himself.

"The fuck you coming in here for?" he said, his voice screechy and peevish, as he attempted to yank up his pants with balm-covered fingers. Flustered, he got caught up in his layers and twisted to the floor as the door opened and Wendy entered.

She approached him with the same expression she had worn all day, as though she required his help but appreciated all that Paul had already done, and that he was under no obligation to assist her further. Seeing this, Paul's fear abated for just a second, and he confused it with hope or even desire. This was enough time for Wendy, with her expression unchanged, to kick Paul in the solar plexus.

He slumped to the floor. While he gasped for air, Wendy rifled through his pockets, but the coveralls confused her search. She grunted and said, "I'm going to need those keys, Paul." Paul did not have the breath to answer, so she kicked him a couple more times in the ribs, neck, and groin. He felt damaged.

She scrunched her mouth to one side and hummed, trying to figure out this problem.

"The keys," she said.

Paul locked onto her eyes as his lungs finally loosened enough to take in air and allow him to think. He fumbled a hand toward his pocket. She sensed his intention, and they slapped each other's hands away until Paul found his mark and slid his finger through the metal ring. He knew the strength of his grip and that she would have to kill him to loosen the keys. The way she continued to kick him made him wonder if that was about to happen. He was too determined to be frightened.

She soon tired and stood over him. Every so often she shook her head as though dismissing an idea. She kicked him again, almost like a question, but did not bother to try to pry the keys loose. She leaned down close, and Paul flinched, anticipating another blow.

"Cubby's going to kill you," she said, stating a fact. She reached down and took off his hat, put it on her own head, said, "Later, baldy," and walked out.

He stayed down, in too much pain to do anything except clutch himself and groan, too afraid to call out. But stimulated. He would fight back if further provoked. Eventually, a guy heading to the bathroom took in the scene: the balm on the counter, this dude on the floor moaning. He called to the bar, "Check out this asshole!" But nobody took him up on his offer. The guy laughed and closed the door.

Paul's phone buzzed. With great effort, he fixed his pants and zipped his coveralls. The bartender helped him to his feet, which sharpened the pain and focused Paul's concern on certain areas, mainly his abdomen and groin, both of which felt as though they were filling with air or liquid. The bartender led him out of the bar and Paul shook off the halfhearted offer of further assistance. His only desire was to leave.

As Paul stumbled down the sidewalk, he saw, through the fading light, that the truck's windshield was smashed. Cracks extended from a hole in the center like lines from a poisonous bite. He would have to keep his head out the window in dog fashion as he drove.

He dragged himself behind the wheel. An organ deep in his midsection that he had never considered before felt torn and broken. The sequence of events looped in his mind. He wished he had said that she was pathetic. That she was obnoxious and sold meth and will probably die soon. That he was better than her, though admittedly it did not appear that way just now. He was, however, proud of himself for holding on to the keys. His hands did not shake when he lit a cigarette.

He checked a new voice message on his phone. Mike again. He said some campers out at Denali called. They couldn't get out because the lot was unplowed. He sounded concerned. "Everything okay, buddy? Oh, and Wilber's fine, I was just messing with you about the hospital. Both our seats were on the ground by the time we got back. You're supposed to loosen the bolts, not take them out."

This unexpected conclusion shook something loose, and Paul laughed until tears rolled down his face, less at the humor than the relief. It seemed to confirm something that Paul's wife had once said, about how those idiots pranked each other because their lives were too easy, and that their tricks prepared them for the harshness of the real world, like how dreams are trial runs for reality. She warned Paul never to prank her because women faced a constant test of all the cruelty that the world had to offer. Not like those rangers.

He drove off, slowly at first, testing his foot on the pedal to make sure applying pressure did not aggravate any internal injury. All was sufficient, and he flipped on the high beams and stuck his head out the window for as long as he could stand it. It was too cold to keep it out long, so he kept his speed down.

Adrenaline sharpened his senses. Everything was in its place. The movie loop in his mind became pleasant to replay. He had not acted perfectly but held firm. He felt victorious, like a poor student who had not failed a test.

Soon trouble was bound to catch up with him. Matters had spun beyond his control. The shattered windshield, the people he messed with, his injuries—all would come with a price. But, he thought, he was strong and good with his hands, and people who can fix things always make their way. He found himself swaying and throwing his fists in pugilistic ecstasy. He rolled up his window, turned the heat on full blast, and tried to negotiate his way through the spiderwebbed screen. He took out a cigarette, pushed in the lighter. As he waited, he glanced in his rearview, which revealed headlights far behind him. He increased his speed. The lighter popped out.

# Perfect Nonsense

### —for Joe

I'm not sure what my grandson does for a living, so I tell people he's a comedian. What type of comedian? they ask. The kind that makes people laugh, I say. But honestly, I'm not sure. Jeremy, how do you make your money? I asked him straight out. He told me he has a prank comedy show on the new website Zonkers.net. I had the girl look up the website for me and there was nothing there, but by then Jeremy had gone home and wasn't able to clarify. When I asked him about it during his next visit, he shook his head like he had never said it in the first place. Fools his own grandmother.

Maybe fifteen, twenty years ago, back when he was a kid—I say a kid, but this happened when he was probably twenty-one, roughly the same age I was when I gave birth to his mother—he'd amuse himself by making me say random phrases to strangers. Nothing dirty or offensive. Simply bits of conversation he wished I had the inclination to say, because if I naturally said such weird things, he'd find it funny that I was so awkward. He also wanted to gauge the reaction of the listener, who was forced to respond to my foolishness, to see if they engaged with me or were amused, or better yet were put off or annoyed. A generous reading of his interest would be that he was a student of human nature. His favorite target was busy people occupied with work—waiters, police officers, flight attendants—because their distraction made them less likely to notice we were joking, plus they could not walk away.

The game began back when he was in college and we drove through Illinois to see a Cubs game—his going to the game with me was my birthday present, though I bought the tickets and drove. During the trip he told me to say to the first tollbooth attendant, *I'll take a Whopper and French fries to go, ha ha ha!* So, of course, I said it, and since Jeremy told me not to drive away after speaking, I fixed a bright, expectant smile on my face as I waited for the attendant's response, as though the guy knew that he was supposed to join in on my witty repartee. The attendant finally grunted and said, *Yep, just like you say at the drive-through.* I thought Jeremy would have an aneurysm from holding in his laughter until we had driven out of earshot.

As we made our way along the tollway, Jeremy worked up an even dumber phrase for me to say to the next booth attendant, who was just trying to do her job. I believe it was, *Is it Friday yet? I hope so because this tummy is rumbling for some pizza, and Friday is pizza night for this za-hound!* We laughed until our faces hurt, and this idiotic game had already made that mundane drive to Chicago more fondly memorable than any family vacation my ex-husband and I ever took with our children. Honestly, I think of those long-ago family trips as pure drudgery. And yet, I could not help but sense a motive—hidden probably even to himself—behind Jeremy's elaborate and hilarious jokes. The pranks seemed designed to take the place of small talk and to curb the possibility of speaking intimately. But on another level, I was conscious that these shenanigans served to deepen and complicate our bond, almost like we were a playwright and actor.

The phrases he fed me became increasingly convoluted from booth to booth. Soon, they turned into rambling comic monologues, and he forced me to commit these insane novellas to memory in the ten minutes before we reached the next attendant. Part of the joke was that he noted every mistake I made and would facetiously and harshly reprimand me after we drove away. I obviously don't remember the word-for-word inanity that Jeremy had badgered me into saying, but I do recall that as the trip went on, he began to sneak personal details into my speeches to help me to remember the wording as well as to stir the attendants' compassion so they would not cut me off. Those intimate details stuck with me, and so I can still basically recollect what he told me to say.

At the last booth I handed the attendant my two dollars and said the following:

> Sir, this glorious morning awaits nothing more than our bounty, and if it isn't too much trouble, I would like to sing to you a song of praise, as I was quite the sultry singer in my youthful days, but I will not sing the kind of praise song you might think, not one to the Lord above or to the sun or the moon or the mother of the earth, but rather one to my dear husband, who has departed us long ago to the world of the beyond, because of his accident—not of birth but rather of the automobile variety—I now have as my ward this beautiful cherub sitting next to me called Mayflower, who isn't really named that at all, his Christian name is Curtis, but Mayflower is the vessel throughout which he first rode in like the pilgrims of yore into my ever-beating heart, which was vacant after my husband drove his heart away in that semi tractor-trailer longhauling a load from neverland to the hereafter, for my heart is now full of Curtis, my Mayflower, and the twist is that my song of praise is not a song at all—no!—but rather he, my darling Curtis, my heart's Mayflower, his presence on this earth is a glorious song of praise unto himself.

Or some such nonsense.

Cars honked behind us as I waited for a response from the gob-smacked attendant. When he realized I was finished, he handed me my change and, with a thick Chicago accent, said, *Okay well, I don't know, I guess I hope it all turns out for you.*

Jeremy twisted with embarrassment for the rest of the drive to Wrigley Field. I shook my head and said, You *told* me to say it! He laughed and replied, But I didn't think you actually would! Then on the walk from the parking garage to the stadium, he thought up an equally foolish thing for me to say to a hot dog vendor. Of course.

Regarding the Mayflower address, I did used to sing in a jazz club and Jeremy was fully aware that my husband—former husband, Jeremy's biological grandfather—was alive and well at the time, working as a long-haul trucker for the Mayflower transit company. Making me out to be a widow was a common ploy to make the listener too uncomfortable to interrupt. Jeremy found it fun to exploit pity.

Recently—this is years later, after my daughters forced me, against my will, to move into *more appropriate* accommodations—the doctor told me I had signs of dementia, and the tollbooth drive immediately came to mind. I pictured myself uttering the same nonsense to the same people except with no control over what I said. The doctor asked why I was laughing. I figured that if I tried to explain about the tollbooths, I might sound even more demented than he already considered me to be. I also would have broken down into a humiliating display of emotion while sitting on a vinyl table in a ridiculous paper gown. Then he told me there were treatments to slow the progression and that I could *still live a full life.* I stopped laughing. More nonsense. I snapped that I did not give him permission to tell anyone. He said he had to tell my caretakers at the home as well as the daughter whom I had at some point given power of attorney. I pointed a finger at him and said, That's on you.

Through threatening litigation, I convinced them to tell the fewest people possible about my brain's forthcoming demise. All I needed was for everyone to start coddling me, appraising my every action as a further sign of deterioration. When I made my stink, I mostly had Jeremy in mind. Receiving pity from the rest of them would be annoying, but their visits basically revolved around pillow fluffing as it was. If my time with Jeremy stagnated in heaviness, though, that would be a true loss.

During his first visit after my diagnosis—though he was unaware of it—he asked me about the other residents, about their quirks. I told me about Sonia, who was nervous about breaking rules. She lived on her own and only visited during the day, so she wasn't alone all the time—

there's a day center where residents and nonresidents can mingle. I explained to Jeremy how, a few months back, they changed the day-center sign-in procedure to a computer system, and ever since, Sonia was incredibly anxious that she wasn't logged in correctly. She went to the director's office at least five or six times each visit to make sure she had been counted.

Jeremy took in this information like he had been dealt a hand of cards. By this time, he's nearing forty—just so we're clear on the age that he's still doing this. After his quick calculation, he said, Here's what you do. Go over and ask Sonia how to work the new sign-in system, say that your grandson is here and you want to make sure he's counted. Tell her that I'm lonely because I'm still single and my career hasn't worked out like I had hoped, so I'm depressed, and the thought that I'm not even counted in this simple and arbitrary way—say those words *simple and arbitrary*—would break my heart like a teacup thrown from a balcony in Marrakesh—those words: *teacup, balcony, Marrakesh*—so you need her to explain to you how the touchscreen works. Only don't say touchscreen, use an overly complicated nonsense term—say *fingerprint identifical touchmount*. Got that? *Fingerprint identifical touchmount.* And then, while she's showing you, always do something slightly different, like always touch the button next to the button she tells you to press, and if she says to type in your resident ID number, you say, *Okay, I got it, type in my Social Security number*, and don't improvise too much, don't overdo it, just keep it simple and act like you understand her, but always do something a little bit different.

He then earnestly asked if I took that all in and if I understood my role. I held his eye and nodded gravely, noticing that he only made eye contact with me while we pulled these dumb pranks. While plotting, he sparked to life, and I felt a true connection. Of course, I didn't mind torturing Sonia for amusement, though I was more worried than usual that I would muddle his instructions, since my failure would signal a more serious concern than simply botching the joke. My biggest issue was that, though I had gone to such lengths to prevent him from knowing my diagnosis, I wanted to warn him that I will soon be worse off than Sonia. I wished I could tell him that in the coming months or years, I'll become too mush-brained for him to pull his pranks on me because it would simply be cruel to tease such a pitiful creature. I had an impulse to suggest that we fill our time with sincerity while I was still able to comprehend and recall what he said. Was it true that he was lonely and that his career was disappointing? Was he depressed? But bringing up our emotions might ruin our inside jokes. He could stop visiting if I didn't go along with these scenes. Anyway, if he was depressed, wasn't it better to join in this moment that provided us both with so much joy, even if it was at poor Sonia's expense? If I was soon to be feebleminded, why shouldn't I perform this hilarious role while I was capable? After all, I was surrounded by people who were itching to tell me about their depression. But none of them could make me laugh.

While I tricked Sonia, Jeremy sat in the corner with a hand over his mouth to stifle his laughter. Every so often I snuck eye contact and felt relief and release, which I chalked up to sharing an exclusive connection, as well as joining in the creation of absurdity.

The last time I saw Jeremy serious was a few years before, when I assumed my brain had plenty of juice, but my knee and my hip forced my family to move me out of my condo. That the state of my body determined where I was to live was a disagreeable concept, and admittedly I did not gracefully accept the change. My daughters bore my arguably abusive displeasure patiently, which made me more expressive.

On the day of the move, Jeremy did not make jokes or propose schemes. He silently lugged my possessions to the U-Haul and then situated my walker in front of my chair. Seeing him so serious and responsible made me feel like I was being taken off to the grave, and I burst into angry tears. He must have recognized where he had gone wrong because he looked panicked and said, It's okay, Grammy, we'll have fun, I promise—remember the tollbooths on the drive to Wrigley Field? Leveraging our good times to usher me through that nightmare had a blackmail taste. I slapped his hand away, grabbed my walker, and made my own way out of my house.

So far, Jeremy has followed through on his promise. His occasional presence has brought me joy. Like old times. People in the home ask me why I act so strangely when he's around and I tell them I don't act any different anytime. Of course, I'm aware that I act like an insane person during his visits. The real problem is when I'm alone. I have never gotten along well with others, having had to make my way in life as doggedly as I have. By the time of my diagnosis, I had become stuck in my ways. As I await the worsening of my condition, I have trouble recognizing if my intermittent cognitive inabilities are derived from my affliction or are products of my own worry. Lately I have begun to wish they would disobey my wishes and let my wider family in on my situation. I made too big a stink to recant my demands.

I sat in the day center and stared out the window, which is apparently what I do now. I'm uncertain what I do when I do this. Perhaps I daydream or watch for squirrels. Lately my mind goes to places beyond my control, and there are better ways of spending my lucid moments than considering the destinations of my wayward attention. Where my thoughts go remains a mystery.

Our new activities director—of whom I am not a fan—shook me cognizant and said to come get on the bus. Bus? She pointed to a bus in the parking lot, directly in my sight line, loaded with beckoning residents of the home. The angry way they waved their hands around, I thought maybe a swarm of bees got loose in there. I asked where we were going. To the farmer's market! the girl said cheerily. I conveyed to her that I've never had the slightest inclination to visit a farmer's market and she showed me a signup sheet onto which my name had found its way. I almost informed her that the sheet was wrong but caught myself. I'd rather spend my Saturday riding that stuffy bus and schlepping around in the heat than admit a mistake to that too-bright-eyed girl.

The bus was full up except for my spot. Depression descended upon me. Not only did I have a miserable afternoon to look forward to, but I had finally become so mentally unsound that I'd forgotten I had signed myself up for this trip. Except then I remembered that Jeremy had visited the week before. Of course! He put my name on the sheet to mess with me. Before then I had only ever experienced such relief upon waking from a nightmare.

Next to me was a widower Scotsman named Iain. It was not worth telling him how I was only there because of my grandson. He wouldn't have appreciated the joke. There's a reason the seat next to Iain was empty. I also didn't want to explain about my dementia, since I might have had to hear about his ailments in exchange. Instead, I laughed, and Iain scooted away from me like I was obscene. He was embarrassed to be sitting next to the latecomer as it was, and now he figured I was crazy to boot.

Tickled as I was that this trip was Jeremy's doing, I wondered why it would have been so distressing if I had put my own name on that sheet and pulled the prank on myself. Was intention the only difference between Jeremy and my dementia? This outlook seemed a bit touchy-feely for my taste—my inclination is to fight these sorts of problems rather than to go with their flow. And yet the idea of a little prankster living within me was an odd source of comfort.

If Jeremy were on that bus, he would have me cook Iain like raw meat. But I couldn't conjure up any nonsense to say to that dour old man brooding next to me in his golf cap. Jeremy had always been the generator and I the vessel. Eventually I concocted an elaborate story about how the queen of France ran a bait-and-tackle shop in her free time. But that wasn't right. I needed to speak sincerely but in a ridiculously convoluted way. The trick was to make myself the embodiment of stupidity and absurdity, a kind of logical vacuum that forced the listener to wonder if such people as me could exist.

Having failed to come up with the perfect nonsense, I kept quiet. The time was not right. I had no clear getaway, like at those tollbooths.

Iain would have asked why I was acting crazy. I stared directly at him as I considered my best course of action. The way he yanked his hat over his eyes and pretended to sleep was a minor victory.

Perhaps one day when my brain is so far gone that I no longer recognize myself, I will understand farmer's markets. Until then, I do not choose to try. From the moment we disembarked I saw no advantage to being there instead of the home. For one thing, the home is indoors and air-conditioned. Another thing, it isn't packed with people who pretend that eyeballing watermelon is a source of fun. I understand that our world lacks zest and sparkle, and that some amount of playacting is necessary to get through one's day. But this was July. It was noon. There was precious little shade. I counted four stands that sold *jorongos*. Okay, I'll stop. I hate farmer's markets. I think I got my point across. But the other people on that bus didn't like them any more than I did. They just didn't realize it. They shuffled along and harvested free samples like a pack of Russian serfs taking in the wheat, wrinkling their noses in open disgust after tasting kombucha or sniffing essential oils or eating a pickled beet. And yet they never failed to amble on to the next booth. Whether this was optimism, boredom, or cheeseparing I don't care to guess.

I wandered alone and mentally tore apart the people who sunburned themselves for no reason, appreciating that I still possessed my powers of discernment. I considered calling Jeremy to collaborate on a scheme to pass the time, but if he was hesitant to help, it would only depress me. It was my job to harness the inanity of the world. I needed to teach myself to cope with dead time before it was too late.

I discovered the one shaded spot in that wasteland where I could sit unmolested and soon became transfixed by a rotund and bearded man rooted in place at his scented-candle stand, which people passed by as though it was not there. Perhaps his candles were in some way inferior. Or his tangled beard and T-shirt that depicted the phases of the moon over an Egyptian pyramid drove people away. Whatever the reason, I vowed to watch him until someone stopped and at least smelled one of his candles. But he was like an apparition that only I could see. Not one person in this overly polite group took notice, and he did not seem to feel the need to hawk his merchandise to entice them his way. Why would he choose to wake up early, pack these heavy candles, drive here, carefully arrange his stock, stand in the sun—why would he even make or purchase the candles if he wasn't willing to try to sell them?

What's that? a voice behind me asked. I was shocked both that some-one was so near and that I had been speaking out loud. And yet I wasn't frightened that my brain had acted outside of my control. The woman who spoke was on the same concrete slab. We sat back-to-back. She was apparently trying, as I was, to stay out of the sun. My heart began to pound as I sensed opportunity. Before I could talk myself out of it, I said:

> My grandson, he comes here with his candles every week because his life isn't turning out how he had hoped, because he had believed himself to be a comedian but soon came to realize that to be a thing means to make a living out of it, and, if you want my opinion, his living is not in the candles that burn but in the candles of the living flame that burns inside our hearts, his name is Curtis and his candle is that which warms me, he is a comedian of the spirit but that will never get you on the late-night shows, because, you see, he is here selling candles for my sake, because his dream has become to soothe my ever-and-lately lonely spirit but not with jokes of the comedic variety, but with money, cash, the hard moola that can buy the wares and baubles that make up a life, which mine has been, so alone first without my husband and now without my Curtis, who, and here's the shocking conclusion, is not a candlemaker at all.

A bunch of dumb words that tumbled out of me in no sensible order. My embarrassment was overpowering, and I had to grip my elbows and force myself not to run away and hide on the bus. The woman was quiet for a minute. I assumed she wanted to get up and leave as well but was being polite because I had said I was lonely. Soon she said, What a lovely story, is that him over there? I couldn't bring myself to speak. I wanted to double over, to hide under the bench. She got up and walked over to the candle booth. It was as though I had moved a solid object using only my mind, which I suppose I had. I never even saw her until she was at the stand. I simply babbled nonsense and she bought a candle.

After the man bagged the candle and took her money, she leaned in and spoke to him. In response he definitively shook his head, which caused his beard to sway. She pointed over to me and the man shaded the sun from his eyes, saw me, and turned back at her as though she might be trying to put something over on him. I should have walked away before it came to that, but I wanted to see what happened, and after she pointed, it was too late. The candlemaker listened more and shook his head again and they both walked over to where I sat. I realized then why Jeremy observed his antics from afar and never became directly involved.

The candlemaker said, Do I know you? And the woman said to me, This is your grandson, you told me this is your grandson. I was about to give up, apologize, attempt to explain, when I saw, behind them, the sprightly new activities director, tagging along with three or four members of our group. The way she held up a peach for the group to observe, as though that peach was so special that it justified the whole trip, infuriated me. I was proud to be part of the hidden faction determined to upset the established rational order rather than to pretend to enjoy living within it. That I discovered this just in time, while I was still able, was a relief, and I was thankful that my affliction would not prevent me from continuing to cause societal disarray, even if I did not consciously disrupt. The rest of my life suddenly seemed tolerable. To the confused strangers, I said, I've never seen either of you in my life, why are you asking me if this is my grandson if he just told you I'm not his grandmother—why are you bothering me? The candlemaker and the strange woman slunk away, baffled.

For the rest of the day, or at least until the activities director searched me out after everyone else was seated on the bus, I inserted myself into strangers' lives, said a bunch of words to make them wonder if the world was slightly misaligned. I got the stand attendants to explain the process of soapmaking or strawberry growing in minute detail, then skewed their instructions back to them so that they wondered if I was hard of hearing or if they had not made sense. About fifteen people searched for my lost dog until someone asked me what breed it was and, as though shocked, I said, Dog, what dog—I thought we were searching for that guy's misplaced *jorongo*? Another time, I asked a man who refurbished bicycles if I could take one for a test ride. I told him I wanted to buy it for Curtis, my grandson, whose car had broken down and, though out of work, he needed a vehicle to visit me at the home, since his visits were my greatest source of happiness. Based on my walker, the man was openly skeptical of my riding ability, and so I asked if he could demonstrate. He mounted and rode down the sidewalk, and when he was just out of sight, I walked away, leaving him to wonder why I would bother to ask in the first place.

# ANKLE GRABBER

When I was sixteen, I visited my two best friends in my hometown. We'd barely been in contact since I'd moved away two years earlier—this was before email and social media—and had probably been drifting apart before that. Even growing up, we had little in common—we had become friends when we were small children, mostly because of proximity. By age fourteen our friendship had become a kind of habit. If my parents hadn't divorced and I hadn't moved away, I doubt we would have still been close two years later. But because we didn't have the time to fall out, I still considered them my best friends and thought it was a good idea to visit. Until I arrived, they seemed keen on this as well, though we had spoken only briefly on the phone.

It may have just been the first time I experienced the particular quality of certain straight male friendships that you should never state your desire to be together. Indeed, one of the first things my friend Albert said to me, not unkindly but more like a psychologist questioning his subject, was "Why did you want to come back here?" I think I blushed and shrugged instead of answering. I couldn't bring myself to tell him that I still considered here to be my home and them to be my friends. I thought that was obvious.

Soon after I arrived, we were joined by my other former best friend, Jake, who had grown bigger and rougher since I'd last seen him. He was drinking a two-liter bottle of Dad's Root Beer and had a large dip of chewing tobacco in his lip. He pretended to be happy to see me, but it was more like he was being forced to spend time with a cousin he didn't know well. Almost immediately, he and Albert began talking about things I wasn't familiar with, and I tried to keep up by telling stories about my new school as though the novelty would interest them. At their suggestion, and with little input from me, we then left to go to a party out in the country. Ostensibly we were going so I could see my old classmates, but based on how quickly our conversation had become strained at Albert's house, I began to suspect they wanted to pawn me off on others since they didn't know what to do with me. For my part, I was glad that I was going to see the people I grew up with again but disappointed that the private reunion with my two closest friends hadn't lasted longer or been more intimate.

When we arrived at the party—a lame, alcohol-free affair that neither of them seemed to want to be at—I was surprised at the group, which was more of a drama-and-arts crowd, whereas Albert and Jake were more the hunting-and-sports type. My friends had most likely guessed that this was where I belonged now, even if they didn't. And though probably they were right, I wished they wanted to share something with me that they enjoyed. I kept quiet, however, and dedicated myself to the task of making a good impression. My return was supposed to be a triumphant homecoming. For weeks I had built it up to myself, imagining that my time away would increase people's desire to spend time with me. In fact, it appeared to have wiped me out of their minds completely. If anything, the guests at the party seemed confused by my presence, to regard it as tedious and unwelcome.

Perhaps the most disappointing aspect of the party was that I had become convinced that returning to my hometown would provide me with the best opportunity I had yet had of losing my virginity. I thought that in my absence I would have gained an air of mystery or just that I would make for a better sexual candidate, since I was only passing through. I went so far in preparing for this likelihood that I hadn't masturbated for five days, a personal record, hoping this abstention would lessen the chance of my having performance problems—something I worried about so much back then that it interfered with my fantasies and I began to wonder if the worry was indeed part of the fantasy, if overcoming the obstacle of my own performance was what I most desired.

It was quickly clear from how the girls at the party refused to look at me that nothing was going to happen and that I had wasted those five days of abstention. My lack of awareness made me ashamed of myself, and I scanned my memory to make sure I hadn't hinted at my hopes to anyone else. Midway through the party, I was already devising a plan for how to sneak away later that night to jerk off into Albert's toilet.

Not long before we left, I approached Albert as he was talking to a girl and I distinctly heard him say *gay*. When he realized how close I was, he couldn't hide the shock on his face. He then chucked me on the shoulder and said, "What's up, dude!" and burst out laughing. Before then I had never even considered the possibility that I was gay, and am in fact not, but the implication, combined with my general feeling of being ostracized by people I believed to be my friends, was enough to make me worry that I didn't know who I was at all. If I wasn't accepted in my own town, then maybe I was also gay. I am sorry to say that the prospect frightened me.

I wasn't sure why I so badly wanted them to accept me again. If I hadn't known them for so long, I wouldn't have particularly liked any of them. My new town was bigger, my admittedly few new friends were more interesting. Yet my old classmates' coldness created in me a deep ache like homesickness, though I still considered this my home. I was, after all, born there.

On the way back from the party, which had been far outside of town, I saw a car sitting off to the side of the road. Not crashed, just parked in a clearing. Albert and Jake hadn't seen it, and I was pleased with myself, since they, being hunters, were usually more observant than I was of abnormalities in nature. My pride manifested itself the way it would in a two-year-old. I scooted up in my seat, pointed out the window, and excitedly said, "Car."

Albert hit the brakes and we slid to a juddering ABS stop.

There could have been anything in that car. It was small—let's say a two-door Honda—and looked drafty and cold, but the windows were not iced over, even though I didn't see any exhaust from the heat running. The hazards were not on. Neat tire tracks cut through the snow behind it. I assumed it was empty until Jake pointed out that no footprints led away from it, so someone must still be inside. If it had been up to me, the contemplation of that car, closed up like a gift, would have been enough. But the characters I was with, guys who were defined by wrestling and hunting and whose inner lives—though I had known them my whole life—were as unknown to me as the identity of the driver, didn't settle for observation. Albert backed up his mother's Suburban and followed the Honda's tracks with high beams blazing. For a minute, nothing moved, and we debated who was going to get out and check.

Then the driver's door opened.

The guy was dead drunk. Apparently surprised by the depth of snow, he dropped to his hands and knees before staggering toward us. We didn't get out of the Suburban. He could have been any of our uncles or a father's friend. Midforties. Combover. Wet patches on his jeans. His puffy coat bunched up, exposing his hairy belly. He was ripe for ridicule, but nobody said a word until he tripped and fell flat on his face and we all started laughing. For the first time since I'd arrived, I felt we were together, that things were the way they had been before I left. The man stayed down, shaking, either cold or crying.

A woman got out of the passenger side, saving us from having to act. Middle-aged, tight jeans, short white coat with fake fur lining the hood, impractical heels, considering the weather. Now I picture her looking as gaudy as a Russian, but it was probably just a special night. She picked her way through the snow and screamed for us not to leave before taking a three-step detour to kick the guy in the ribs. As she turned away, he grabbed her by the ankle. His hand, illuminated by the

Suburban's headlights, appeared too white, almost blue, against her red-heeled boots. We caught our breath at his unexpected dexterity. Looking back, the gesture was more pathetic than malicious. But his hand might as well have been a bear trap, the way she yelled.

Whether out of basic midwestern heroism or the more fundamental midwestern desire to justifiably beat someone up, we all three opened our doors and stood just outside the car. The guy—I saw now that he was crying—immediately let go and sunk back down into the snow. I remember hoping his coat was pulled down, because the idea of snow freezing his belly gave me the creeps. I turned to survey the others through the open doors of the car. They had started their prefight jittering and were ready to move on him, though he had released her. I wanted to advocate restraint but knew it would make me sound weak. Plus a part of me wanted to see them put this man in a chokehold, though normally violence didn't appeal to me. I knew I would even join them in the beating if it came to that, no matter how disgusted I would feel with myself afterward. I couldn't bear to be left out of anything else.

Instead the woman strode past me and blundered into the back seat, yelling for us to close the doors, turn up the heat, and get her the fuck out of there. Outranked, we relented.

Once moving, we didn't say a word, only listened as she asked herself orienting questions aloud.

"What the hell am I doing in here? Who the fuck are these boys? What are they, fourteen? Can that one even drive?"

We were just as confused as she was and stayed quiet. For my part, I recognized this as an opportunity to reassert myself within the group, to justify my being there. Her presence in the car was a gift. The novelty of the situation put us back on equal footing. I tried to think of some way to be the leader of the expedition. I considered myself the most worldly and mature, since I lived in a city now and read books and wasn't on the wrestling team and didn't hunt. But all I managed to do was occasionally make eye contact with Albert as he drove, our slight gestures communicating a mix of anxiety that we might be doing something

wrong by ferrying around this drunk woman and some shared if un-
spoken hope that the encounter might turn sexual. I justified my inac-
tion by telling myself that the time was not right, that I was waiting for
an opportunity to arise. Even my eye contact with Albert, this tenuous
connection, was a small victory, though, after a day and night of feeling inadequate and left out. Still, I made sure not to let the look linger,
remembering how Albert had said I might be gay. The fear I felt at the
party returned, so to disavow him of this idea, I got his attention, nodded toward the woman, and surreptitiously made lewd motions with my
hands and tongue, though this was something I normally would never
have done. He laughed, and I hoped I was in the clear.

Meanwhile we drove on through the increasingly heavy snow. We
passed a cow, I remember. It was standing at the edge of the woods,
with no farm around for miles. It looked lost. We all loved it. We were
equals in our amazement and all had our theories as to why it was there.

Seeing that cow must have allowed the woman's thoughts to come
around to acceptance, but she still didn't stop talking, and never spoke
directly to us. "So this is a damn hoot! Look at these little guys. Bunch
of boys!"

With the snow still falling, and having seen that cow, and listening
to the woman's steady stream of questions and exclamations, and with
the prospect of sex existing only in my imagination, I believe this middle section of the ride was the best part of the night. I was aware of a
harmony settling over us. It reminded me of a common scenario in my
house: my parents, back when they were still married, calling a truce
in a fight so that we could eat dinner as a family, and how, during the
meal, something—a nostalgic reference or the simultaneous recognition
of their kids' innocence—would cause them to glance at each other
and grin.

In the meantime, the woman was giving us directions. We ended
up at a crooked little ranch-style house a few miles outside of town.
When Albert pulled into the driveway, she got out without a word and

we watched her walk unsteadily down her unshoveled, icy front walk. Surely Albert and Jake felt the same sense of loss and relief that I did.

Then she turned around and said, "Well, come on, ducklings!"

We obeyed. The interior of the house was brown and moist. She turned on all the overhead lights so it was bright as a doctor's office. There was precious little decoration. The only adornments were a free bank calendar and a Miller Lite clock that did not tell accurate time. Her TV was gigantic. We sat down with our coats still on. She disappeared into the kitchen and came back with a big plastic bottle of vodka and placed it on the table in front of us. It was depressing, that big, cheap bottle. It reminded me of when I used to stay overnight at Jake's house—before my parents forbade it—and how his alcoholic father and uncle drank the same brand of vodka. I once saw his uncle mix it with ice and milk and gulp down an entire glass for breakfast. Now, I helpfully unscrewed the cap but did not take a drink. We all stared at the bottle as though expecting it to start the conversation. The woman sat on the very edge of the couch, as if she was ready to spring up and run away.

Now that we were all in front of her, and seeing us in the light, she seemed to be trying to figure us out. She was scrutinizing us, sizing us up. Wrinkling her forehead, she lit a cigarette and did not offer us one. The way she studied us, you would think she was judging us for a prize. She gave each of us the onceover, one after the other, from feet to crotch to chest to forehead, giving little nods, questioning looks, and private laughs. This allowed me to assess her as well. Perhaps a hard thirty-eight. Crinklingly attractive in a way I like now but did not consider one way or another then. She scooted up to the coffee table and took a gulp from the bottle. We followed in turn.

One of us—let's say Albert—then started talking about something embarrassing, something schoolboyish, let's say a high school wrestling tournament he had recently competed in. I tried to catch her eye, let her know that I was aware this was not what you talked to adults about.

You talked to adults about jobs and mortgages, about movies and books.
You had sex. What I really wanted her to do was line us up and tell us
what to do, or, better yet, do things to us. Take out our cocks and get us
all off at the same time, one in each of her hands and one in her mouth.
That this fantasy came to mind confused me—I had never before had
any desire to share a sexual experience with other men. But I got an
erection right there, thinking about the three of us lined up against the
wall with our pants down, her confident hands on us. I actually had to
hold the flaps of my coat together over my crotch to hide the bulge.

I probably just wanted a group activity, anything that would bring
my friends and me together and also fulfill my desire to finally have sex.
To combine the two would make it an occasion so momentous that we
might never talk about it again. It actually brought to mind a similar
situation Albert, Jake, and I had once shared: the time we all masturbated on the same couch while watching Cinemax at Jake's dad's house
the summer before I moved, when we were all fourteen. I remember
I was the last to finish, and when I went on too long, Albert sleepily
growled, "Will you just get it over with?" So I pumped harder until I
did, unspectacularly dribbling over my fist and onto Jake's dad's scratchy
basement couch.

But sitting there on that woman's couch, I was mostly thinking about
how my erection was proof that Albert was at least partially right about
my being gay. He had known me almost as long as I'd known myself.
Maybe with the added perspective of distance, he saw something in me
that I had missed. I didn't know any gay people, I didn't know much
about gay people (I was sheltered, and this was the mid-nineties), I
only knew you didn't want to be one. Perhaps, I considered, I was bi.
At least then I wasn't doomed to a life of having sex with men.

I knew I didn't have time to figure this out just then. So while Albert
was going on and on about his wrestling match, I came to a strange
agreement with myself about my sexuality; I told myself it would be
okay for me to be gay (or bi) as long as I never admitted it out loud and
could still have sex with and fantasize about women. It was basically a

way of tabling the discussion. Here and now was not the place or the time for self-discovery. (It was only later, after I gave it a thorough going-over, that I determined I was indeed straight; oddly, when I was alone, the realization carried a sense of loss, as though I'd missed out on a unique experience.)

With my sexual identity momentarily squared away, and since the woman obviously wasn't going to line us up and get us off, I decided that I at least wanted to establish a special connection with her, to let her know that I was more capable and adult than my companions and to reassure myself that the reason I didn't fit in anymore was because I'd outgrown them. Sure, having sex with her would have been nice—sex would have been definitive proof that I was not gay and that my friends were the deficient ones. But based on her body language, sex seemed a distant possibility, so I focused on making a good impression. I didn't know what Albert and Jake were thinking, sitting there looking puffy and young in their letterman jackets. I did know that, as a group, we weren't doing well.

So I interrupted Albert's wrestling tournament story.

"Who was that ankle grabber?" I asked.

"Ankle grabber?" she said.

Everyone laughed. She made a terrible, harsh, grating sound—the sound of a shovel mixing concrete with too much gravel in it. Jake and Albert, though, laughed almost in harmony, and to my ears it sounded like relief, as though they had been holding in laughing at me all day and had only now found an outlet for it. I was hurt and baffled that they were all so quickly unified. I knew what I'd said was perfectly fine—even now I'm on my side here—but the room was against me, and I didn't know how to recover. That my friends displayed such open joy in taking her side about a small, unfunny mistake was a clear signal that they were done with me. Until then they'd at least attempted to hide their contempt. It occurred to me that I was now officially alone, that I didn't have anyone in my new town and I no longer had friends back in my hometown, either. But instead of handling this with grace, I plunged on.

"No," I said. "I knew that was a dumb thing to say. I was just kidding around. Remember when he grabbed your ankle?"

My friends howled at this, though I knew they didn't know why it was funny. Neither did I, honestly. "You just keep holding your coat together, all right, honey?" the woman said, at which they howled more. A sensation like falling came over me and I thought of the man tripping into the snow. In a desperate attempt to regain some status, I took a deep pull from the vodka bottle. "Aw, poor little ankle grabber," she said when I coughed as the last bit went down my throat.

How many nights did I stay awake and go over "ankle grabber" in my head? It haunted me for years. Each time I thought of it, I reasoned it out completely and always concluded that, at worst, what I'd said was mildly stupid, that I'd overreached while trying to sound clever or something. But it wasn't worth what I got. "Who was that guy driving the car?" was all I had to say.

I went to the bathroom and hoped that by the time I came back, her spotlight would have landed on some other prisoner fleeing the yard.

It did, in a horrible way. When I returned, Jake was sulking alone, holding the bottle of vodka on his lap like a mother gorilla guarding its young. Albert, he informed me, had been taken away by her, to the basement, to help her move a chair.

This killed me. And to make things even worse, I was now too afraid to speak. I felt I had no control over the meaning of my words. I wanted to say something that put the circumstances into perspective, that showed that Albert, though chosen, was not better than me, that his being chosen proved his inferiority in the long run. Instead, all I did was dwell on my defeat in silence, allowing my unhappiness to sink in and solidify, like a fossil being encased in plaster. Jake, with his glugging, was no help. To myself, I made fun of her free calendar and beer clock while I listened for any sounds coming from the basement.

Albert! I mean, of course she hadn't picked Jake. He wrestled heavyweight, had acne, Skoal was bulging from his lip. That he had not been chosen, either, was no consolation. And while I could have at least made an effort to get him on my side, to seek solidarity with him in our both having been left out, I had no interest in that. I didn't want to be lumped in with him.

"She didn't even talk to you once, did she?" I said after a few minutes. Jake drank heavily from the plastic jug.

Not long after that, Albert came running up the stairs and, without a word to us, bolted out the door. We chased after him. It was wonderful.

Albert said nothing as he drove. We begged him for details—anything. To my consternation and delight, he was sullen and silent as he drove doggedly back along the same route, the roads becoming thicker and thicker with snow. If he had been forthcoming with details—even if about a failed attempt at sex, or something banal, like that they'd actually moved a chair—it wouldn't have given me nearly the same joy as his silence. I assumed he was so deeply hurt that he couldn't speak. I believed him to be humiliated into silence. This belief filled me with a satisfaction that I imagine usually comes only with the delayed gratification of recognition after a long and arduous career—like a great old actor finally winning the Oscar after being passed over many times. Yet his withholding was frustrating as well, and despite not wanting him to speak, I desperately wanted to know what had happened, as, clearly, did Jake. So we kept badgering him until he saw that cow again and swerved across the lanes toward it, as though he wanted to jump the ditch and hit it, but then he swung back when we screamed at him to stop. After that we shut up.

It was still snowing when I saw the Honda in the distance. I had become unfamiliar with the roads since moving away and hadn't been sure where we were going until it was in sight. For some reason I was not surprised to see the little car, which was now covered in a kind of cocoon of snow. And though he had been, in a way, much discussed back at the house, I hadn't thought of the man's actual body since we'd left him, not until the car was once again in view. I should have been worried about him the whole time. Now I became frightened that my thought-lessness had made me partially responsible for his death. I imagined inches of snow on top of his prone form, that coat still rolled up on his chest and frostbite burning his stomach. Perhaps, I remember thinking, he was so covered by the snow that it protected him, like cryogenic freezing or when people live for days after being swallowed up by an avalanche.

As we neared him, I began to wonder who he was, this bald, fat man who drove a lousy car. This man I never wanted to become. For some reason I assumed he was married and seeing the blond woman on the side, that they had gotten drunk together at a bar and were on their way to her place when he lost control or realized he was too wasted to drive. I don't know why I thought this—maybe it was the way she kicked him, how that seemed too harsh a reaction to his car breaking down. It was more like the release of frustration that comes of unrequited love or pent-up disappointment in one's own life. It does occur to me now that perhaps the woman made such a big deal about my "ankle grabber" comment in order to deflect having to define her relationship to the man. It may have been my question, and not its phrasing, that cut too deep.

But when Albert parked down by the Honda, the only sign of the man was some dragging footsteps—as though he hadn't had the heart to pick his feet up all the way—leading from his crumpled imprint to the road. I let out a sigh of relief. Albert punched the steering wheel.

What happened next I'm not proud of. When I tell it to people, which I rarely do, I play up alcohol's role, but really I only had a couple of swigs from the jug. And since I wasn't drunk, I wish I could at least justify what I did by saying that I went along with the others because I wanted us to be united in a destructive act. But I wasn't thinking that at the time—I wasn't thinking much of anything. Really, back then, I just didn't respect that people existed when they were outside of my field of vision. I didn't know the value of property, since I'd never had to support myself. I was a little prick. It's not an excuse. It's the opposite.

What I'm trying to say is that we bashed his Honda with whatever sports equipment Albert had in the back of the Suburban. Baseball bats, golf clubs, a hockey stick.

I don't see the act corresponding to what I now think of as "fun." We were perhaps looking to take out our aggression on something, or trying to prove ourselves capable of action, or we simply saw a car we could destroy and so we destroyed it. It was like we were accomplishing a task we were always meant to accomplish. I somehow felt both more in control of myself and more uninhibited than I ever had before or have since. I assume that I only felt this way because I was first humiliated, then liberated from my misery by a worthless and hurtful act. I'm worried that this reveals a defect in me. Even now I'm not ashamed of what I did as much as of how good it made me feel to do it. This may be why I have since tried at all costs to avoid embarrassment, because I now know that the simplest remedy to that kind of discomfort is violence, which I will later regret. It seems like an unsatisfying cycle I have been wise to avoid. It's the illogic of the domestic abuser. The fact is that it makes my stomach burn to think that this person lives inside me, that I might still be capable of such meaningless and selfish destruction.

It went how you'd think—smashed glass and thumping aluminum, shards reflected in the SUV's headlights. I wanted to see a window shatter, so I stepped back and watched Jake take out the back driver's side with a bat. I remember that he hit it methodically—no pleasure, no passion, like a lumberjack getting the job done. We swung and swung until there was little left to dent or break. Albert then grabbed a bowling ball he had bought at a thrift store but never taken out of his trunk, walked up onto the roof of the Honda, and threw it down with both hands. It made a perfectly round hole in the spiderwebbed windshield and disappeared into the interior. For the first time since we left the house, Albert's expression changed. He looked like a boy whose balloon had just floated away. I told him I would go in and retrieve it for him, but he shook his head and said we should go.

Just one more thing about that ankle. Though my mentioning it at the woman's house that night troubled me for much of my late adolescence and still makes me cringe, I don't think I picked out that detail by accident. That fat hand around her ankle made a stronger impression on me than anything else that night. The image comes unbidden in times of pain. Like just after my mother died. That moment, in the headlights. Stuck pathetically in the snow, he makes a last-gasp attempt to hold on to her. I'm not sure I have ever given that effort. I tend to position myself to avoid the possibility. I am nearly that man's age now. It's not a mystery to me how he felt when he discovered his ruined car. I do wonder, though, if he remembers grabbing on to that ankle, hearing her scream—if that made it clear that something was over and there was nothing more he could do.

# WIND

In Senegal, Ndiaga Diop never drank. He didn't much after he moved to America, either. But last night one of his fellow mailmen had his bachelor party and Ndiaga, never having been witness to the tradition, took part despite having to deliver mail the next day. Now his head hurt, his body trembled, and as he bent into the wind that whipped down the street into his face, he wondered if his bag had always been this heavy.

The yards of the houses he delivered to were mostly brown, and some were littered with things like dolls and lawn ornaments in various states of decay. The houses themselves seemed to be falling apart. Despite this, Ndiaga liked his route. When he started, he was warned by other mail carriers to be careful, but Ndiaga so far preferred this neighborhood to the rich, well-tended ones that were quick to make complaints.

The night before was a blur. Sour-throated, he tried not to recall specifics. Of course, it didn't matter what he wanted because he couldn't remember anything. Such forgetfulness was a blessing. His only goal today was to make it to the next house.

The wind gusted and dirt hit his arms like slingshot pellets. A young tree bent nearly double. Metal clanked rhythmically. Ndiaga was blasted so hard by the air that he almost forgot how bad he felt.

He had never wanted to get his shift over with this badly. Most days he lingered, stopped to kick soccer balls with children or help steady a ladder. But today, between the wind and his hangover, he was later than he had ever been. Still, he cared about the quality of his delivery. Ndiaga hated very much to get complaints.

As he approached 310 N. Clay Street, he noticed they had painted their shutters again. Where there had been sunflowers there was now a rising sun on one shutter and a moon on the other—amateur work skillfully done. Ndiaga was not sure if the young, excited homeowners were indecisive or if such rotation was planned to keep their style fresh. Perhaps the next time he saw Claire Wright, who was the younger, more responsible one, he would ask her. Usually, he and Claire conversed amiably for as long as it took him to walk backward down the front walk and over to her neighbor's house. The other woman, Naomi Kessler, he saw less often. Once she was lounging in a lawn chair in the front yard, feet in a kiddie pool, and when Ndiaga walked up to the house Naomi raised her beer and said, "Yah mahn, come and have a beer after you deliver your mail, mahn," in a fake Jamaican accent. Ndiaga never knew what this joke meant.

While he recalled this strange and probably racist joke, a particularly violent gale dislodged a letter intended for Naomi from Ndiaga's hangover-weakened grip. Honestly, if it were presorted, Ndiaga would have waved off the letter as a lost cause. But his brief glance at the return address had revealed it to be a possibly important, even governmental piece of correspondence. So he took off after the letter, which had caught a current and was ducking and diving down the sidewalk like a low-flying bat.

Almost immediately after he began to run, the wind blew Ndiaga's cap off his head, careening it into the street and making it roll brim-to-back down the road like a tire. There was no decision. Ndiaga did not want to pay for a new hat.

Hat recovered and tucked safely away in his mailbag, Ndiaga angrily stuffed 312 N. Clay's mail into the box and then shook his head.

"I was a doctor in my country," he said out loud.

After he said it, he smiled. He had been a mailman there, too.

~~

Jared had been paused on top of the hill for some time, surveying the houses and bulging, big-leafed trees below. Over to the right was a large store called Mattress Factory and in the distance was downtown. He shivered as the wind whistled and streamed itself through his jeans and thin nylon jacket. The surrounding light was orange and the air smelled like walnuts. The sign at the bottom of the hill had read "Sled at Your Own Risk," and he only walked up to see how things looked from the top. Far below, a man sprinted crazily down the middle of the street, as though trying to escape this wind. Other than that, the view was as motionless as a painting.

Jared was inexplicably envious of the running guy. Seeing such desperate movement made Jared want to keep on his way. He was always jealous of people with a purpose, though he also believed that indifference about his future positioned him for interesting things to occur. He was excited to have finally arrived and the sprinting man's determination further spurred his hope. And yet he stood still. His only nod toward effort was that he leaned against a stump that he could have easily been sitting on. Instead, he rested his bag upon the jagged, ax-cut wood. His bag was the size and shape of a punching bag and green. He suddenly became frightened because he forgot how he ended up standing on this hill.

He was going to his uncle's house. That was as far as he had planned. The hill was a side trip. Not having a clear idea of where to go next felt right. His uncle was the one who told him that real experiences happen when you don't worry about consequences. That knowledge had been imparted to Jared when he was nine and he never forgot it. Once he even considered getting a tattoo that said something to that effect, but he couldn't figure out how to word it and got a lightning bolt instead.

At a corner store he bought two twelve-packs of Miller Genuine Draft, a Rice Krispies Treat wrapped in plastic wrap, and a pack of American

Spirits. The cigarettes were unopened when he arrived at his uncle's house.

He set the beer down and knocked, looked off into the street. Leaves and garbage blew by at high rates of speed. Plastic bags. The sky lost its orange tint. Turning to the door, he knocked twice more and saw a button for the doorbell and pushed it.

Jared sat alone on a brown couch. The basement was fixed up with two recliners, the couch, and a large tube TV. Jared respected the bare walls, how his uncle didn't feel the need to advertise his tastes. Such self-containment was in line with Jared's own thinking, and he nodded at the walls. His uncle asked him what he was doing that for.

Soon his uncle, whose name was Mike, Uncle Mike, came back in, drinking a Schmidt's beer. They didn't have Schmidt's in Oregon, where Jared had just come from. He heard they had stopped making it completely and relayed this secondhand knowledge to his uncle.

"Schmidt's? Of course they still make it. Why wouldn't they?"

"I haven't seen it in a while is all," Jared said.

Uncle Mike blinked hard and shook his head.

"So, Oregon?" Mike said.

"Logging, yeah. Real good up there."

His uncle looked away, drank his beer.

"Made a bundle," Jared said.

Mike sighed and rubbed his eyes, leaned forward. His striped pajama bottoms hiked up to reveal thin ankles. The hair on them looked matted down, wet. His uncle's ankles reminded Jared of the bare walls except that the sight of them left him on the verge of homesickness.

"Sorry I barged in like this," Jared said. "You said before I could come stay anytime. Thought it would be cool to up and do it, you know. I took the bus all the way, got out a few times, got a hotel, hit up a bar. Gets lonely up there at the camp."

"I just woke up," Uncle Mike said. "But it's okay."

"I won't stay long."

"No." His uncle appeared ready to say more but stopped.

"I tell you my brother's getting divorced?"

Mike looked at him steadily and said, "How could you have, you just got here?"

That night they sat on the back porch and smoked. It was screened in, and the wind blew through it in high-pitched yelps. Sitting with their backs to the gusts, they looked out the side of the porch, directly into the neighbor's kitchen. A woman kept coming in and out, cleaning, getting a snack, doing a dish. Every time she came in, she turned on the light; every time she left, she turned it off. Jared meant to count the number of times she did this because there was nothing else to do.

"Maybe she's OCD," Jared said.

"What?"

"The woman."

"Who?"

Jared looked at his uncle. "Your neighbor. Doesn't she come in and out a lot?"

"Of where?"

Mike rustled around in the cooler and took out a Genuine Draft. When he saw the two cases on the porch earlier, he had said, "Brought enough for an army." Now he said, "You know I got my last unemployment check today?"

Jared didn't answer. The woman had just turned on the kitchen light. She went to the center of the room and pulled the cord on the ceiling fan. She pulled it again. And again. After each pull, she watched to see if the fan was slowing down or speeding up, then finally stood there longer to see if it would stop altogether.

"I was thinking of spending it on apple trees," Uncle Mike continued. "You know, you get the trees, sell them. Like door-to-door. Was thinking how I could plant them for the customer and everything, right there when I sold them." He looked over at his nephew. "Does that make any sense? Apple trees?"

"Yeah," Jared said. He was fascinated by the woman. She seemed pretty. The idea of her seemed pretty. Her whole house was dark except that room where she stared directly above her at the ceiling fan.

"Maybe you could pitch in, buy some trees," Uncle Mike said. "You're a good-looking kid, you could go out and sell them, and I could plant them. I mean, you could call me at home, and I could come out. Do the planting. It's legit. Got a buddy who can get me all the trees I want."

Jared put out his cigarette. He didn't like smoking in the wind. He couldn't feel it when he inhaled.

"Guess I don't know what I'm doing now," Jared said.

"Could be something, the trees," Uncle Mike said, nodding.

Jared moved forward in his seat. The woman looked down at the floor, then out the opposite window, and then, without looking up, pulled the other cord on the fan and the light went out. Jared said, "What if we did it? Got a truck. A business license. Teamed up. I got money. Don't want to go back with my folks. They told me not to. Nowhere better to go."

"A truck?"

"We'll need one. And a garage." He looked away from her darkened kitchen, toward his uncle. "You imagine it, we could get a decal on the truck door and everything."

His uncle picked at his lip, looked away.

"Just what is this?" Mike asked.

"A plan."

"I got a check for two hundred eighty-two dollars. You're talking about a truck. All I want is to sell some trees, make some money. Not start a whole outfit."

A long moment went by, and his uncle lit another cigarette. The shock of the sound and the spark made Jared jump.

"So, the trees, yeah. Door-to-door. That could work," Jared said.

"Forget it."

Jared waited for the light to turn back on. Mike's head snapped out of a nod. "God I'm tired," his uncle said. "All the time now. You'd think not working for this long I'd be as wired as a lemur." Jared wasn't listening. Nothing made sense. Two splinters pierced his skin. Uncle Mike began to snore. The kitchen light came back on.

~

When she saw glittering eyes in her headlights, she figured the raccoon must have escaped the rain. All day she had thought it was raining but it had only been wind. Now it was 3 a.m. , and the wind was dying. She worked as a cleaner in an office building downtown.

The raccoon mesmerized her, and she kept her car running, even though the garage door was shut, to keep from breaking the spell. Her foot held steady on the brake and light reflected red behind her. She did not look directly at the raccoon cowering next to her landlord's paint cans, since eye contact might scare it off.

The automatic garage light clicked off. Lucy did not have a next move. She put the car in Park and eased her foot off the brake. An animal should not be stuck out in this weather against its will. While cleaning at work, she often wished there was a dog around, so she had something to talk to—she pictured a medium-sized white dog. Someone was inside the house. Her roommate. The rent was cheap. Lucy had lived here for four months, her first time away from home. The raccoon gave a start or maybe shuddered. Lucy waited for the door to the house to open, but it never did.

With the garage door down she could only idle for so long in that suffocating place. She saw a garage window was cracked. So that was how the raccoon got in. Her car rumbled and clanked.

If the car exhaust were to kill her, she figured, the last thing in the world she would see was the chassis of her ex-boyfriend's dirt bike. The chassis is the frame. It sat on the table below the raccoon's shelf. Her boyfriend had used her garage to fix his bike. The chassis looked unable to support the pounding it took on those dirt tracks. He had raced on Saturdays until his bike conked out.

She shut off the car. The headlights stayed on automatically for thirty seconds and the raccoon, in response to this jolt of silence, leaned away from a paint can, eyes locked onto the light, as though anticipating the start of a race. Before the headlights switched off, it slipped behind the shelves. Smoothly. Like being flushed down a drain. Lucy thought about getting out, cornering it, but didn't.

The wind had stopped. It was still as a stone. The backyard was lit by distant streetlights. Around her were little rustlings.

"Raccoon?" she said out loud.

Tree branches littered the street, but the wind had swept the yard clean, made it look fresh. Like a field for planting. Even the leaves, piled in drifts against the fence, looked right, as though they might break someone's fall. She went to the back fence to check if there was a hole under which the raccoon might have snuck.

Most nights—even nights sans raccoon—Lucy came out here. Her sleep schedule was off. Lately she woke at 8 p.m. Since the breakup, even on days she didn't work—Tuesdays and Wednesdays—she spent much of the night in the backyard, at least if her roommate was home. She ate snacks and looked at her phone and dozed in the padded chair until 7 a.m., when her roommate went to work.

How she lived, sleeping like that, made days seem not to exist. She went to bed in the hopeful part and woke in the decline. But it was not forever, and for now the altered perspective made her feel smarter and more aware—or at least different and deliberate. Yesterday, for instance, as she took a walk in the wind before she went to bed, she watched some boy standing atop the sledding hill, just staring down, for a long time, and she was fascinated that he did not know that she existed. Scattered as her brain had lately been, she considered hiking up there just to let him know she was down here, and somehow that fantasy filled her with hope. The desire to approach the strange boy on the hill was what she thought about as she continued her search for the raccoon. It provided an irrational reason to seek answers to this mystery.

"Raccoon?" she said, quieter now.

Searching along the back of the fence—or at least strolling along with her eyes on the spot where the wood disappeared into the dirt—

she thought how not long ago she lost a pair of valuable earrings that her grandmother had given her. Her ears were not pierced then, and still were not, and her grandmother gave them to Lucy, her only granddaughter, to entice her to pierce them. Her grandmother had said that she would look even lovelier.

While the image of the teardrop emerald was firmly in her mind, the wind picked up, and she ducked her head and closed her eyes. Squinting through whipping hair, she saw leaves float, swirl, plaster against the fence. The gust engulfed her like a current, without clear beginning or definitive end. When she realized it was over, she shivered though she was not cold.

Nobody understood why she kept the earrings in the box. She never so much as held one to her lobe while looking in a mirror. Her brothers said she should sell them. But she was pleased by their potential. They were not merely objects worn or sold. She did not attempt to explain this because the idea was not clear in her head. All she knew was that she had liked that they were hers. As she walked, the security of possession came back to her, and she brushed her fingertips against her earlobes. A year after she last looked at the earrings, just before leaving her parents' house, she found the box in its familiar place in her dresser drawer. It was empty.

The gate leading to the yard next door startled her. She snapped to attention and, without considering the consequences, opened the gate and stood on the neighbor's grass. Why the gate existed she did not know. This was the first time she had gone through it.

"Raccoon?" she whispered just to make sure.

There was silence.

She hunched against the fence and held perfectly still. At work she did this in the stairwell and had the same feeling, like she was stealing something. In the middle of the yard was a plastic, sun-colored play set, turned over on its side, probably by the wind. She bet that if there was a swing on that play set that it had swung like crazy in that wind. All over town empty swings must have been flying.

She wanted a proper glimpse of her neighbor's yard, so she closed her eyes to allow them to better adjust to the darkness. She used to do this back when she slept at night. Closed her eyes as long as possible to allow her pupils to dilate and then open them to see what her room looked like in the dark. Though just as often she fell asleep before she had the chance.

With her newly attuned eyes, she saw it was not a play set at all, but a yellow machine, a trowel, she thought it was called, with arm and toothy bucket poised above a hole. Beside the hole was a tarp-covered mound of dirt, domelike in the dark. Perhaps the hole would someday be a swimming pool. She smiled, thinking how she might hear them splashing and shrieking while she tried to sleep during the heat of the day.

⁓

"Honey!" Naomi Kessler called from the porch. "Honey, look at this."

She held a filthy unopened envelope over her head.

"What is it?" Claire asked, concerned but wary, as she hurried through the living room wiping dirt from her hands. She kept her bare feet on the carpet and rested her hand on the doorframe over her head. Naomi became distracted by how, with sun framing her as it was, Claire looked like a swimming trophy.

"Letter in the mailbox," Naomi said, slapping it into the palm of her left hand.

"So?"

"It's Sunday!" Naomi said in disbelief.

Claire shook her head and walked back to the kitchen to continue working on her flower box for next week's craft fair.

To Naomi, the presence of the letter bordered on supernatural. She checked the mail four times yesterday. She had not been expecting a letter, but the crazy wind had made her want to step outside and join in such extremity, even just for the time it took to check for mail. The rattling windows had made Naomi feel cooped up as she assisted Claire with her crafts. Twice Naomi had remarked how she had never seen such a punishing wind before and Claire said it was not *that* bad, and that anyway a person can't *see* wind. The letter, which appeared to have dragged itself out of a shallow, wet grave, seemed to somehow prove that Naomi's assertions about the wind had been correct.

She sighed, went back into the house, and sat down. She wanted Claire to care more about the letter. Naomi did not care in the least about the flower box but had still asked questions about it and complimented the quality of its construction. Naomi happened to place more importance on the uncanny than on craft projects, and for whatever reason it is acceptable to openly discount that which is difficult to explain. A dog barked outside, and Naomi leaned forward on the couch, raised her chin, but couldn't see anything out the window.

The envelope was addressed to Naomi. The paper was smeared with dirt and warped and puffy from water. The return address was washed out and obscured by filth. A water-stain line cut down the middle, between the *o* and *m* of her name. The letter must have spent the night in a puddle. It was dry now.

"Looks official," she said quietly.

An unopened letter could be anything. She covered the return address with her thumb to thwart temptation. Long ago she had learned to appreciate the benefits of delayed satisfaction. It was her father who had taught her how the hope of waiting nearly always surpassed the reality of the outcome. She had been a restless, impatient child, and his lessons were meant to instill patience. This was why he always spent two weeks building up their every-other-weekend visits. He would call nearly every day and get her worked up about the gifts he bought for her, the trips they would take, the candy he had shipped in from Europe. And then they would spend every weekend the same way: sitting around his apartment watching TV and eating hot dogs. When he dropped her home on Sunday his standard joke was, "At least you got to enjoy all that other stuff in your head!" Somehow this did not damage her. She took pleasure in both the thrilling fantasies and the comfortable reality.

The sound of hammering came from the back room.

"Why is it here now?" Naomi called out.

The hammering paused.

"And why would I check the mail today?"

The hammering resumed.

She wanted to tell Claire how it felt like yesterday did not happen at all but saying that out loud would not have made sense, even to Naomi. Then, as though confirming the reality of the previous day, she recalled how the wind had blown Claire's homemade weathervane off the roof, and it tore into their neighbor's siding. Naomi had not yet spoken to this neighbor, and she would surely be responsible for the damages, though Claire was the one who had poorly affixed the hen-shaped vane. Such was Naomi's role in the relationship. She sighed and reached a finger under the flap of the letter.

A knock on the door so startled Naomi that the letter fell from her hand. She picked it up before answering.

On the porch stooped a hulking old man in a too-tight brown linen suit with frayed cuffs. His eyes were trained straight ahead, a little over Naomi's head. His nose was like a turkey baster bulb.

"Yes?" Naomi asked.

"You get it?" the old man asked eagerly.

"Excuse me?"

"The letter?"

"Yes!" Naomi cried, holding it up.

The old man wagged his head. "Found it nearly a mile away. Damndest thing. Sitting ass-up in my birdbath."

This was turning out to be an even better story than Naomi had imagined. Well, maybe not better, but equal.

The old man continued. "Dropped it off a couple hours ago, went and had myself a coffee and a couple Danish at the bakery around the corner. Nice place. Greeks, I think."

They gazed at the back of the envelope. Naomi dismissed the idea of thanking the man. They were in accord, and such gratitude would only serve to shift roles.

"Think I should?" Naomi finally asked.

"Your letter. Was just in my birdbath." He said it again with such wonder.

Naomi nodded.

"No wind today," the old man said after a long moment.

"I know," Naomi said. "Really something yesterday. Maybe the strongest wind I've ever seen."

The old man grunted. "It was up there for sure. Seen some real gales back in my Canada days though."

"Okay. I'm going to open it," Naomi said.

"Good plan."

"Probably just a bill anyway."

The old man scoffed audibly. "Isn't a bill," he said.

The glue pulled off easily and Naomi, with a certain flare and ceremony, shook the letter from the envelope so that it fell into her hand. She folded the empty envelope and put it in her back pocket, as though she meant to keep it as a souvenir. The paper crackled when she straightened the letter. She read it to herself.

"Dang it," she mumbled, frowning.

The old man kept quiet.

Naomi read on and soon glanced up and blushed.

"From the city clerk's office," Naomi said, and continued to read.

During the ensuing silence the old man picked up an ashtray on a nearby table and dumped it over the railing into a thriving garden next to the porch. The ashtray had been filled with dirt.

Naomi considered this an overly intimate thing for him to do.

"My business license was denied," she said.

"On what grounds?" he asked, wiping dirt from his hands.

"Zoning," she said.

"They give you back the application fee?"

"There's no check enclosed," she said.

"Maybe they'll credit it back to your account," the old man said with genuine warmth.

"Maybe," Naomi said quietly.

It took everything the old man had not to ask what the function of the proposed business had been. He decided to wait her out.

"It was for my dad," she said. "He wanted me to file for his business license. He needed it in my name."

The old man stayed silent.

"Plowing," she said.

"Snowplowing?" he asked.

She nodded. "Apparently, since I wrote down this house as the business address, they worry about the trucks being parked on a residential street."

"Makes sense," he said. "But plowing's a good business if you got the equipment."

The screech of a car stopping short made them both turn and search out the sound.

"Funny thing is," she said, "I knew they would turn it down. Obviously, you can't run a snowplow operation out of a residence."

"Certainly wouldn't want my neighbors to do it."

"I didn't make a mistake," she said, not listening. "I just didn't want to be in business with him. Don't want to be tied to him, financially. Taxes and all."

"Get your name on paperwork and you can get screwed out of house and home." He badly wanted to ask if her father was a shady character.

"He means well," she said. "And it would have made me some money. He *said* he was doing it for my benefit. It just seemed like a hassle. But now that it's rejected, I'm worried I need the extra income."

The old man made a sound with his throat.

"I'm a little stretched, to be honest," she said, glancing over at her neighbor's house.

The old man wanted to give her some advice about money. Something to put her mind at ease, like how money comes and goes or how it is people who are truly important. But he did not believe any of that.

"Anyways," Naomi said.

"Well, okay then," the old man said.

"Thanks for bringing it back. Better to know."

"Anytime. Even if it was bad news."

"Yeah."

"Name's George by the way."

"Thanks, George."

Naomi closed the door.

George began walking in the direction the wind had blown the day before. There's one mystery solved. Satisfying outcome too. He bet that girl's father was a real rascal and she was covering for him. Who has their daughter apply for their snowplow license? Rascals, that's who. A good guy would make the money himself and cut her a check. George was freshly thankful that he had lived his life alone.

As he walked, he remembered that girl in his backyard last night, just leaning against the fence in the dark. George could barely sleep anymore, and the girl provided welcome diversion. At first light he ventured out to make sure she hadn't monkeyed with that little excavator the power company set up back there. That's when he saw Naomi's letter, ass-up in the bird water. Gave him some solace that the girl in his backyard had caused no trouble. He hoped that she had stowed herself away back there solely for the adventure. Best part was that from now on, because of her, when George was caught in insomnia's grip, he had a reason to turn off all the lights and stare out the window, to see if that neighbor gal popped over to get herself another look.

Though the scenery around here was unimpressive, and George was not the type who gained comfort from familiar sights, he slowed his step to delay reaching home. He thought how the key to longevity was to seek mystery, and that night would come soon enough.

# Pharaoh

One night when I was eight years old, I couldn't sleep. All of a sudden I didn't know who I was. Staring into the blackness it didn't make any sense that I existed, so I went to the bathroom and checked the mirror to make sure I was really there. My father came in and I didn't cower. I turned to him with what I imagine was the same dazed, slightly cross-eyed look I had been giving myself for the last twenty minutes.

"In or out," he said.

I calmly told him how it didn't seem possible that I was alive. He nodded. Then he stepped onto the shaggy bathmat with me and gazed into the mirror. Even then his face was saggy, like small invisible weights were attached to the spot between his cheekbones and eyelids and to the underside of his chin. In the reflection I could see that his bathrobe was tied tight, militarily smart, and his usually neat hair stuck straight up over each ear like the beats of a heart monitor.

"That'll happen," he said, as though speaking to himself in the mirror. He did not fix his hair. He looked down at me and said, "Go to bed. You'll forget about it in the morning."

I stood there, fascinated. Then I went to bed. That is the best memory I have of my father.

There were seven of us in the house. Three boys and two girls and my parents. Growing up we lived modestly. My father worked for Mutual

Life of Des Moines—doing what, I never knew. I assume he assessed claims. One night a week during the summer we went out for ice cream and every spring we went camping. As far as we knew we weren't different from anyone else.

My father never asked us a question. He believed everything in life should be sure and held every idea with the conviction of a zealot. Hard work was sure, so we all worked like pack mules as soon as we were able. My brother Steve made me get up at five in the morning every day of the Iowa State Fair so we could get the best spot to shine the shitty boots of the farmers walking in the gate. We immediately handed in our take to our father, as nothing in life was a free ride.

His surety made us believe him. It also made us frightened of him, as it left nothing for us. He was going to invent great things and make a million dollars; in his previous life he was a pharaoh; Richard Nixon was the greatest president of all time. We had no doubt these were facts as they were impressed upon us since birth, and even after we figured out that they weren't true, we desperately wanted to believe them.

Though he expounded on his ideas at the dinner table or after ordering us to roof the house, he never taught. Anything said was simply a sounding board for his views because nobody else would listen to him. Steve told me after we were grown that he heard my father call a conservative radio show every Sunday night, then slam the phone down when the producer wouldn't patch him through ahead of everyone else. Mostly he was quiet though and spent his nonworking hours in the basement or watching the news, cursing under his breath anytime a Democrat was mentioned.

Once when he got a new drill, my brother Keith approached him and asked, "What are you going to make with that, Dad?" and my father snapped back, "Get out of here, you rat!" Often, we would have to hold back our tears until we reached the kitchen, which smelled of baking meat or cabbage and potatoes, and our mother would hold us against her apron and tell us in her soft Scottish voice that our father was a very busy man and needed to be left alone.

Recently I got a call at work and assumed he was dead. The authoritative voice on the phone said, "Is your father Alan Reilly?"

"Is he dead?" I asked, only briefly looking away from the email I was reading.

"Well, no," he said, and cleared his throat, "but he has been arrested."

He was sixty-five and arrested. I had never so much as gotten detention in school. I asked what was required of me. I had to go to Omaha and get him. I asked what he did, and the officer said, "Why don't you just come to Omaha." I lived in Milwaukee by then and after I hung up the phone, I called my wife, who told me I had to go.

"Come along," I said. "God knows he likes you more than me."

"He does not. Anyway, what about the kids?"

"Leave them. It'll be good for them. Make them appreciate us being around more when they starve for a night."

"They'll burn the house down."

"Even better, we can collect the insurance and live it up on some beach for a while."

She laughed, then said, "No, he's *your* father."

Four years after I questioned my existence in front of the bathroom mirror, I bribed my sister to take over my paper route for a week. I was twelve and, even then, it seemed strange to take time off work. It was midway through the last summer that I was still on the good side of boyhood, a time when I thought of nothing more than sports and fishing and riding bikes, and I went with my friend Tim Connoly's family to Clear Lake. Every day we waterskied and then ate steak or shrimp cooked on the grill by his father. One night we had a dance contest that I won after I dressed up like a mummy and danced to "Walk Like an Egyptian."

When Tim's dad drove me home afterward in his Lincoln there was a U-Haul in front of our house. My brothers and sisters all had boxes in their hands. It was July fifth. Tim's dad said, "I didn't know you were moving," and I said, "Same here." Before I even got out of the car my father yelled at me to drop the luggage and pick up a lamp.

We rode to our new house in the back of the U-Haul like refugees getting shipped to an even lousier country. Linda took Karen, the youngest, into a fort they had made while packing the mattresses, Keith sulked on the couch as it balanced on the wheel well, and Steve and I sat huddled between a desk and the thin line of light that came through the rattling door that we hoped was latched properly.

"What's going on?" I whispered to Steve.

"Dad quit his job three months ago and hasn't been making the house payments," he said.

"How do you know?" I whispered.

"He told us this morning. Said Keith had to go get the truck and we had to be out by five. Then I asked why, and he said it. Said he's not going to work there anymore. Mom started crying."

I nodded like it was something that happened every day and kept all my other questions to myself. A box fell and we could hear the muffled crunch of glass breaking inside of newspaper wrapping. Karen wailed from deep within her mattress fort. After a minute Steve said, "Dad knows what he's doing."

"Energy bags?" I asked.

My father and I were in the car after getting a lecture from a very understanding sheriff's deputy. He informed me that this was the last break for my father and from now on he would be treated as a common criminal. Then my father had to say he would never do it again. So, he said, "I will never place another one in any government building in Omaha." And the deputy said, "Anywhere." My father said, "Anywhere in Omaha." The deputy said, "Anywhere. Or you will go to jail." My father said it.

"Without color the world stops. With more color and more *force*" —he emphasized *force* so much that his whole body jerked in the passenger seat of my Taurus—"the world works harder, it drives, it moves forward."

"Maybe, Dad, but you can't go into a government building and put bags of colored beads in the air ducts."

"You don't think productivity would have increased?" He rubbed his hands together briskly and placed them on his bright plaid pants. I looked over and saw his blue-striped shirt had multiple stains that still had the shape of movement, like they had just dripped and dried instead of being wiped away. "It's those bleeding hearts who are trying to tear down this country who stopped it. They know the truth and are using it for themselves."

"You're lucky you're not in prison right now. The district attorney could still press charges."

"They wouldn't."

I knew it didn't do any good to press on. Anyway, I didn't care. It felt like a speech I'd give my kids if they got in trouble for something I myself didn't have a problem with. There was nothing for me to understand; I would have been more surprised if he hadn't done something like this.

After a minute of listening to the air rushing in the windows he looked at me and said, "Why aren't you at work?"

"I had to come up and get you."

"What? That's ridiculous. You should have told them no. You're important. They can't get along at that place without you. You make it run."

"Well, Eileen said I should."

"She said to? I thought she knew better."

I went to see a shrink once and they gave me a questionnaire that asked if I loved my father, and it struck me that I never even considered it. I checked no, of course, but I would have also checked no if it had asked if I hated him.

The psychologist was Eileen's idea, and I had no intention of going. "Life isn't easy," I told her. "If it takes going to someone else to make it right then it probably isn't going to actually be right anyway. Besides, I can fix myself."

"That's exactly what your dad told me when I brought it up to him," she said.

She told me once that people bristle when I come in the room. Her word. Bristle. I didn't give her the satisfaction of admitting it was true, but the thought of putting anyone through that frightened me.

The truth is that sometimes I can't help but come home from work and pause and sigh before opening my door. All day I'm in meetings or reading briefs or talking to coworkers, wanting to be home and then I get there and realize it isn't as satisfying as I imagined it. And then I started hearing the snap of silence when I opened the door. I've known that silence my whole life. The talking stops and the TV stays on just like it did at five thirty every day of my youth, that is, until my father quit his job. My sister would get so nervous at around five fifteen that she would watch TV from the hallway until she heard the click of the door and slink away before he saw her.

The new house my father moved us to was about the same except we didn't own it and it was in a worse part of town. There was a tree in the yard that sprouted hard, green apples and the shutters were orange, but that's all I can remember that separated it from the other places we moved to after that.

There was no way of telling if quitting freed him enough to reach his potential. We never did see anything he invented. Later in his life he claimed to have invented those convex mirrors that bulge out of the rearview mirrors of semitrucks, but I investigated it and learned it was patented in 1954, when he was eleven years old.

Not that he was only an inventor. He was more of an idea man. There was one whole semester in middle school when I told all my friends that we were getting a new Mustang after my father announced the news at the dinner table. I even wrote a report about it, giving a history of the car and writing about my dad's benevolence. My teacher gave it a B- and in red pen wrote that I shouldn't get my hopes up. Then one Saturday my sister got the mail and among the mountain of third and fourth notices was an envelope with the return address from the Ford Motor Company. She handed it to my father as though she were feeding a crocodile.

"Idiots," I heard him mutter after he read it.

Later that night I got out of bed and fished the envelope out of the trash. It contained a form letter that informed the Prospective Advertiser or Promoter that the Ford Motor Company does not accept unsolicited advertising or other promotional materials and that they thank him for his interest in the Ford Motor Company. They included his letter:

Dear Sirs,

I have YOUR new advertising slogan. In a recent issue of *USA Today* I read that the sales of your iconic automobile the Ford Mustang are, to say the least, waning. Well, congratulations because I've solved this little "problem." All I ask in return is one new Mustang, paid in full. I am so sure that you will use this slogan and want to keep me on at least in an advisory role that I will include my slogan herein. My only fear is that one of your "lackeys" will steal it before it gets to the proper decision-making body or to Mr. Ford himself. Be assured that I have a copy of this letter in my files. Your new slogan: "Drool Your Way to a New Mustang." My address is printed above.

Your Future Colleague,
*Alan Reilly*

I crumpled it up and placed it deep into the trash and muttered, "Idiots," though I couldn't muster the same indignation as my father.

On the drive to Omaha, I resolved to speak honestly to him. That was another thing Eileen had told me on the phone. She said that I had to go and bail him out and that I at least had to say something to him. If I didn't, she said, I would burst. Lately I had been bursting more, bursting like a dam, over things I didn't really care about, like the kids eating too much candy or the cable bill. Bursting was the other reason she said I should see the psychologist.

But it's easy to resolve to do something when you're driving alone through Wisconsin and Illinois and Iowa in the summer. There is absolutely nothing more certain than corn fields. So straight and uniform, so square. It's all green and blue. Out there I couldn't imagine bursting and I could imagine having my say. But out there I didn't have to see the guy. I might as well have decided to yell at concrete for being so difficult to dig into.

She told me to see the psychologist after one of those evenings when I came home from work and everyone looked up at me like I was an intruder. I remember sitting on the edge of my bed, still wearing my work clothes, thinking how it would make more sense to me to put my shoes back on and return to work rather than to walk into the living room and relax.

Instead, I rallied. Something sparked in me, and I decided I'd play pickle with the boys. Run them ragged, maybe tear a hamstring. Let them rip up the yard and, when it was all over, enjoy a moment of boyish togetherness when Eileen halfheartedly chides us for wrecking the grass. I imagined us smirking, glancing at each other out of the corners of our eyes, three boys sent to the principal's office but there together. Hell, even just pulling out the baseball gloves and plastic bases for the first time that spring seemed enough to make it worth it.

They were still slouched on the couch, watching some show that involved kids their own age doing magic or playing music or something.

"Off the couch, we're going to play pickle."

They groaned. "It's cold out," Jack, the older one, said.

"Yeah," Max chimed in. Neither of them looked away from the TV.

I scanned the room, looking for the remote to shut it off and force them to play pickle with me for god sake.

But, before I could, Eileen came in the doorway from the kitchen, drying her hands with a towel, and said, "Boys, go outside and play with your father." She gave them a hard, knowing look with her eyes.

"Forget it," I said.

"No, they'll go," she said, nodding at them.

"Forget it!"

They all gaped at me, and I went off to my office to act like I was busy. I flipped on my computer and my eyes strayed out the window to the front driveway, where the basketball hoop stood solidly. The net, frayed by winter, flapped in the wind. I thought how Jack was right. It probably was too cold to play baseball.

A minute later I turned back to my computer and instead of my desktop screen there were lines and lines of seemingly random text. I hit a button and then another and each time I did, more letters, numbers, and symbols filled the screen. I pounded individual keys: Enter, Backspace, Delete, Esc, Esc, Esc, Esc. More lines.

I spun my chair and thought about yelling for Eileen, as I assumed she infected my computer. On my desk was a pen set I had received for my birthday, and I picked up the heaviest one, held it in my fist, and tapped it against the glass top of the table next to my computer. Harder and harder I tapped and finally lifted it an inch higher, brought it down, and the glass shattered. Eileen ran in and screamed when she saw a small cut on the bottom of my hand bled onto the shards.

That night in bed she held my hand and covered the two stitches with her thumb and told me to see a psychologist. To see one, or she would leave me.

A couple weeks after I read my father's letter to Ford, I told my mother I was too sick to go to school. She felt my forehead, frowned, and said it was cool. But I had never missed a day of school, so she believed me, she just said that it's worse if you feel bad and don't have a fever.

At ten that morning my father got up and showered and when he saw me on the living room couch, he gave a start and said, "What are you doing here?" I told him I was sick, and he said, "Right on schedule." He always said that. If we broke a plate washing the dishes or spilled our milk or didn't make the baseball team it was always "Right on schedule."

And because there is nothing to say back to this, I stayed quiet and turned back to *The Price Is Right* and tried to look sick by opening my mouth slightly and placing my tongue just inside of my bottom lip. After inspecting me from the doorway for a minute, he went in and ate the three boiled eggs and half a grapefruit my mother had prepared for him that morning.

It was strange being in the same room alone with him. It hardly ever happened. Usually, we anticipated it and steered clear. But this was part of my plan. I wanted to see what he was. In the weeks since reading the letter I had been having a fierce debate with myself over whether his slogan was worthy of a Mustang.

I pretended to watch Bob Barker and Plinko but really focused on my father. His breakfast took no more than three minutes. He placed a whole egg in his mouth and chewed hard, then put the next one in before the first was finished, and the grapefruit could not have been eaten louder or faster if it had been eaten by a toothless dog. When he finished, he wiped his mouth and the crumbs fell onto his shirt. His mouth was still covered with flecks of egg and pulp. He got up without so much as a glance down at the mess he had made and went down to the basement.

For an hour I heard nothing. None of us had ever been down there. We assumed it was full of wondrous things that would remake the world. The silence did not reassure me. It was not the sound of innovation, of drive. I was so unnerved that I stole out of the house in my pajamas and crept to peer into the basement window. The windows were covered over but some tape had come loose on one of the newspapers and I caught a view inside. There was no movement, and I wondered if he was down there. Fear began to grip me because if he wasn't there, he could be right behind me. I imagined his hand clasping my shoulder like he was Freddie Krueger.

Then there was a twitch. I saw him lying on the floor staring at the ceiling. Newspaper covered my view but after repositioning myself by putting my head upside down into the dugout window well, I could make out some sort of a chandelier or baby mobile above him with crystals dangling around a light making rainbows that refracted across the walls of the room.

As I crouched there spying, he sprang up and beelined to the steps leading up to the house. Scrambling, I made my way to the front door, and as I got in, he was already upstairs and looked at me without recognition. I never considered offering an explanation. All he did was fill his pockets with almonds from a big bag in the cupboard and leave the house.

His route was indirect. Once he made three lefts in a row and then stopped for four minutes to stare at the base of a tree. I timed it with my watch. The park where he ended up was only about six blocks from our house, but it took almost a half hour to get there. And though I was always at least a block behind him, I could tell by his gait that he was a man who had somewhere to go; he had already started wearing his red-and-yellow plaid pants, but he could very well have been walking up Madison Avenue in a steel-gray suit.

The park where he ended up was a rundown strip of grass, a place our mother forbade us to go after dark. Homeless and ragged men fished for dinner in the small pond. Later, in high school, I learned that it was a good spot to buy pot in a pinch.

By the time I arrived, he was already among the group of men congregated on the benches around a bird-shit-covered statue of a warrior holding his sword high in the air. I was struck for a moment by how strange it was to see my father around other men his age. Even before he quit his job my parents never spent time with their peers. He seemed at home though. There were four or five of them and they greeted him with claps on the back and handshakes. I heard them call my father "Pharaoh" and one called him Akhenaton. Their laughter rang out through the park.

I sat back on a bench near the pond where I could sneak glances from time to time. They wore multicolored clothing, two had beards that went down to their chests, they were pretty filthy. At home my father was the great man he believed himself to be: the unquestioned pharaoh, all-knowing and in control. But here, set against these men, I only saw a man without a job. I imagined passersby wondered if there was a mental institution nearby. I wasn't bothered by it. It felt much the same as when I realized there was no Santa Claus. There was no regret or sadness. One day you are old enough and just figure it out.

On the way into his apartment, we talked about my job, and I told him I did some outside consulting on the side. "You should charge a hundred dollars an hour," he told me. I told him I charge a hundred and thirty. "You should charge two hundred!"

"Sure, Dad," I said, as I opened his door.

His apartment smelled foul. Fruit flies swarmed. Food decayed in the overstuffed garbage cans and the smell of stale old-man sweat emanated from the piles of clothes spread around the floor. There were half-eaten plates of food on the tables, an open bag of potato chips on the couch, and spilled chocolate milk on the countertop that had congealed.

"Is this how you live?" I whispered.

He didn't say anything.

"Linda said she came and cleaned three weeks ago," I said. "And what about the maid service we got you?"

"Maid service? Please, man. I'm not going to have someone come in and do what I can do with my own two hands."

"But you don't. Of course you could do it, it's simple and necessary, but you don't," I said, my voice rising.

"Calm down. There's no reason I can't. Or else Linda will come back. You people today are too concerned with things that don't matter."

"But it matters, damn it! It's unhealthy. It's not right. Just do it for Christ's sake or else use the service we gave you, but don't act like you're already doing something."

My therapist told me to see the goodness of the everyday. Not the goodness of every day, but of *the* everyday. Every day would not be good. It can't be. But life doesn't have to be disappointing because it isn't interesting enough.

Soon after she told me this, I took a vacation from work and didn't tell Eileen about it. For a week I woke up and showered, ate, joked with the kids, played with the dogs, and drove in the direction of work. Then I would turn away. The first day I spent at the movies. I watched three in a row and called and said I would be home late. When I got home, I worried she would smell the popcorn on my clothes.

The next day I drove. Four hours in one direction and four hours back, stopping once in a farm town to eat a small feast at a diner. That night I was exhausted and heard Eileen tell the kids to let me rest because I had a tough day at work.

On Wednesday I realized that I wasn't doing enough. If that was all I could do to fill up my days what was the point? I spent the entire morning parked outside my office in my work clothes trying to think of something to do. Then I remembered I had an appointment with my therapist that afternoon. I told her what I was doing, and she paused for a moment before saying she thought it was a good idea. Then I asked what I should do with my free time, and she shrugged. She said that I shouldn't worry about it.

The next day I started trying. Pretending I had to go in early, I left around dawn and drove out of town. It was November and very cold but still I got out and walked to a small pond I saw during my trip on Tuesday. Staring at it, the stillness, the surrounding woods, and hard, flat fields, I tried to conjure up feeling or thought. There was a ring of ice around the edge, and I stood there throwing rocks, trying to break holes in the ice.

My father and the strange, scraggly men stayed around the park for most of the day and soon I moved to the opposite side of the statue to hear what they were saying. I wasn't worried about him catching me; he hardly saw me when I was in the room.

"Chi? Ha ha! Okay, okay, if chi is energy, then it's the body that is the producer."

"The body? Have you been listening, sir? The body is a conduit."

"You said the world is the conduit."

"The body is the conduit into the life system, that's totally different from the energy of world. You know that!"

"The world! Have you ever even seen an electric current?"

I had no idea who was speaking, and it didn't matter. I liked them. I found myself a little proud of him, just as twenty years later I was proud of my son when he told me he was going to pray at the foot of a dead raccoon until it came back to life.

At three o'clock I had to leave. My brothers and sisters would be home and if I wasn't sick on the couch, I would never hear the end of it. As I tried to sneak away, my father spotted me.

"Why are you just standing like that?" he barked. I was frozen mid-stride after I made eye contact.

"Hi, Dad," I said.

He was too enthusiastic to glower. All he said was, "My son knows. Robert, what drives the world forward?"

"Work," I said cheerfully, happy to be in the clear.

"See, even he knows," he said, and threw up his hands. "Love? How could you be so naive, man?" A man with dark glasses who was smoking a pipe shook his head sadly at my father's question.

My dad walked home with me. We took the same zigzagging route back and he didn't say a word until we were two blocks from the house.

"What do you think about evolution?" he asked.

"I don't know."

"Well, come on! Do you know what it is?"

I said I thought so.

"I just have a hard time believing I come from a monkey."

I nodded up at him, even though I wholly believed I could.

Two weeks later we moved out of our house in the middle of the night.

We drove to the Olive Garden in his white 1989 Cutlass with license plates that read PHARAOH. After our fight about the mess in his apartment,

I had given up and watched a Cubs game as he napped, and we hadn't spoken since except to decide where to eat. I was too keyed up to have a talk with him. It made me angry that I flew off the handle while he stayed perfectly calm.

The restaurant was brightly lit and the tables were filled with old people. There was a wait because a tour bus on its way to Branson stopped and deposited a load of seniors. We sat at the bar.

"You're drinking wine now? Do you know what that does to you? Cranberry juice. That's what you should drink."

I nodded and took a gulp.

We sat in silence for a moment before he leaned over conspiratorially. "Will you look at all these people?" He turned in his seat and laughed too hard; it didn't sound like real laughter. "Gads, man. They go where they're put."

"They're just eating dinner like us, Dad."

He flicked his hand like he was swatting a cup of water onto someone's lap. "They're weighting down the world. Dry, colorless, things. This is exactly why we don't *progress.*"

I opened my mouth to defend them again but then wondered why. If Eileen and I were there alone I would make fun of them too, knitting their brows over whether the chicken cutlet comes with a vegetable side and shaking their heads at the waitress for not bringing enough breadsticks to their table.

"How would we progress otherwise?" I asked without thinking.

He squinted at me as though he had never seen me before. I kept my eyes off center and held him in my peripheral vision.

"*Progress.* We can't keep on this way. Unless people start acting like human beings and figure out what's really happening, how the world really is, we'll never get out of this"—he struggled to find the word—"*rut.*"

Taking another drink of wine, I smiled and wondered why I had never wound him up like this before. "Suppose they did start acting right. Or properly. If we just got up on these seats and explained the facts to them about how the world is and they all believed it. What then? I mean, what would come of it?"

His look was priceless. Pure incredulity.

I kept on. "Pure, full, earthshattering enlightenment in this Olive Garden? Would we all see our past lives and would the skies open up over our heads ready to deliver us to exactly where it is we were always meant to go? Something to make it all worth it?"

Wrinkles formed on his face in ways I had never seen. Creases of joy. He opened his eyes wide and said, "Exactly! I've been waiting to hear someone say that!"

I began, "No, Dad, I was just . . ." But I cut it short.

This one I'd give him. Anyway, I supposed it counted as having a talk.

Sitting at the table a few minutes later, watching his bald shiny head jerk around the air like he was following a fly's path, I became suddenly optimistic. Perhaps someday I could explain the real facts. Put into words how I was alternately terrified and jealous of him. How I admired him for the very thing I loathed him for. One day maybe I could tell him that I do actually understand that the world should be how he thinks it is: that we should all be former pharaohs; that being in the proximity of bags of colored beads should make the world run more efficiently; that we should be able to make our families support us so we have a shot at doing something truly worthwhile, even if we don't know what that is. I'll say how it was almost worth it that my brothers and I had to make car payments and that my mother had to work two jobs just so we could stay in houses that were never big enough. At least we gained a genuinely unique take on the world.

I know, I'll tell him. I know how you feel. Every day I have a different opinion of how you lived your life. But it means too much to me, my family. They might not put up with what we put up with. If they did, sure, I could see doing it. But I'm not as certain as you, I'd say. Maybe while we talked, I could sit there like a statue too and we could just say words to each other and, for a moment, be the only ones who knew what we were talking about.

I still go to the mirror sometimes. In the middle of the night when I can't sleep. I look at myself bravely, but I can't quite see what I saw when I was eight. Not that I know anything more now, but it isn't desperate like it was that night. Now I look at myself and listen to the sounds of my house and sometimes I open the window in the bathroom and feel the night air. I do this perhaps twice a year now. Every time I do, I hope one of my kids will come in and ask why he exists. If he does, I'll tell him to go to bed and that he'll forget about it in the morning.

# Scorch the Earth Beneath Your Feet

I was commissioned by an insurance company to make a road safety film to scare their drivers into being safe. Though I suspected it would be used to screw their customers in some way—that they could, for instance, deny them coverage if they had not watched this film prior to getting into an accident—they paid me four thousand dollars and gave me a thirteen-thousand-dollar budget, plus a car to crash. I was in no position to refuse.

My film school friends, with whom I am in contact via a WhatsApp group, were all very supportive, though they are all too big now to have to do piddly-shit projects like this to pay the bills. One of them directed six episodes of *The Bold Type* and now has secure work in the TV-directing game. Another's art films have been screened in galleries, and because of those was tapped to direct an episode in the final season of *Transparent*, and now has her first feature in postproduction. Another directed a couple of cult-successful indies and was offered to direct the next Amy Schumer movie (which she initially turned down because of implausibilities in the script, until the studio upped the offer). The most successful one made a short film that won an Academy Award, and after a successful first feature, was recently tapped to direct a super-hero movie.

I had only mentioned my insurance-film job as a joke, but they all responded enthusiastically (two of them texted, "You're going to kill it!"). They thought it was all I deserved. I'm sure they all texted about my failures in a separate WhatsApp group, one that I imagine they created to chat about lame California-rich-person bullshit without making me feel left out. I wanted them to laugh and tell me to refuse to do the movie, though I had no choice. I wanted them to make a joke of it, even though I'd probably end up depressed and take their jokes as a slight.

Honestly, though, the movies and TV shows they make are pretty awful. I would never say that out loud. At most, I half watch their corporate bullshit while I scroll my phone, and only then so I can plausibly profess my admiration for their work. So while obviously I wish I had their successes, and I wish that I wasn't embarrassed to talk about myself at parties, and I wish that I was financially secure—I'm not jealous. I want to have what they have but I don't want to be them. If one of them, now, risked their commercial comforts by creating something that had a chance to fail and ruin them, if they put something on the line—only then would I truly envy them.

You know what I *would* admire? If someone took a shitty insurance gig and then wrote a script that was way too ambitious. And if that person meticulously storyboarded it with the same effort they would give as a DP on a Kelly Reichardt film. And if that dumb project kept them up at night. And if they became so invested in the insurance-film character that considering her grief brought tears to her eyes. And if, after all that, they were fired by the insurance company for taking too long and for being too ambitious. If they were left with nothing except the memory of effort. I suppose that what I admire most is the willingness to scorch the earth beneath one's feet.

So, my friends' support, though it angered me, also ended up inspiring me to make the most of the project. Perhaps it could be like how Kiarostami started out making government-commissioned instructional films for children in Iran. Or how Barbara Loden made educational shorts after making *Wanda*. I didn't text these comparisons to the group. But hell, what did I have to lose? Why make *less* of an opportunity? Four thousand bucks could fund a short film on a shoestring budget. Do the festival circuit. My friends, despite all our shit-talking behind each other's backs, would gladly provide contacts for me, make calls on my behalf—they really do want what is best for me, as I do them.

I went to my college film lab. An old professor of mine took pity on me and shared the lock code to the lab on the condition I don't rat him out should I get caught. I had attended the school twelve years before and do not currently teach there, though I would happily adjunct for peanuts. Instead, I freelance local commercials, I shot and edited YouTube pranksters' and influencers' videos until TikTok pulled the rug out from under that market, and I have—under a different name— filmed weddings and bar mitzvahs.

At the lab, I discovered some old Carl Theodore Dreyer informational films commissioned by the Danish government in the 1940s. Dreyer, Kiarostami, and Loden—not bad company for the instructional-film genre. Dreyer made one about getting checked for cancer, another about Danish churches, and—bingo!—an eleven-minute road safety film called *They Caught the Ferry.*

The film only has about three lines of dialogue, about how the man and woman must hurry from one ferry to another. Much more time is dedicated to the ferry docking. Almost seven minutes to the front wheel of the motorcycle, power lines, and the man's face before a truck—driven by Death—runs them off the road. The last thirty soundless seconds are of the ferry leaving without them, followed by a wooden dinghy holding two stark white coffins, steered by an old man with a long beard.

How was I supposed to compete with that! The form had been perfected in 1948, apparently. I couldn't even borrow from it since the film is so rarely seen. Watching it put me in a funk for about forty-eight hours. But then I considered that Dreyer was already famous when he made those shorts. He *chose* to make them. He had already made *The Passion of Joan of Arc* and thought of these films as an opportunity to expand his oeuvre. I mean, I didn't exactly do any Dreyer research beyond scanning his Wikipedia page, but the timing would suggest he saw these government-commissioned films as an opportunity.

I picked myself up, dusted myself off, and returned to the film lab. I rewatched *Two-Lane Blacktop*. Then a Chinese film with a forty-one-minute handheld take from the perspective of a man on a motorcycle called *Kaili Blues*. Also, for the popular perspective, I watched *Mad Max: Fury Road*, *Gone in 60 Seconds*, *The Fast and the Furious: Tokyo Drift*, *The Cannonball Run*, *Smokey and the Bandit*, *Baby Driver*, and *Drive*. I watched some Kiarostami, for those shots of clouds reflecting off windshields. I watched Hitchcock and fell in love with back projection. *Il Sorpasso* because it ends with a car crash. So many movies made by and starring men. Women's cars break down, or they are more inclined to walk and bum rides like in *Vagabond*, *Wendy and Lucy*, and *Wanda*, which are far superior films.

In a drunken fit of inspiration, I fired off a 3 a.m. email asking the company for a twenty-five-thousand-dollar increase to my budget. They gave me an extra seven hundred and moved the deadline up a month.

Road films are perhaps the opposite of road safety films. The links: a driver taking a risk, usually a crash, and an emotional reaction. Often a villain. Except for *Kaili Blues*. I couldn't bring myself to do one long take though. The form is too associated with *Birdman* now. That macho Iñárritu stuff isn't for me.

My limitations, imposed upon me by the insurance company: the crash must involve an uncontrolled intersection. There must be at least one death.

I wrote the first draft of my script in a furious forty-five-minute spree. It was returned with the note: "We don't want to give them nightmares." This led me to believe I was on the right track.

My second draft, in progress, which will surely also be rejected: A woman of talent. Opening shot of unmade bed in foreground, evidence of unrecognized dreams—a sculpture or something—in background. We suspect it's a room in her parents' house—it's a small bed, trophies and ribbons on a shelf. Pillow shots of smokestacks to establish middle America, power lines to evoke driving and connection (also homage to Dreyer and Ozu), an empty uncontrolled intersection. She's out to lunch with her more successful friends. Her clothes aren't of the same quality; her eyebrows twitch when they order more wine "for the table." She gets a text: "Remember, pick up Matthew at three." It is almost two thirty. They begin to pour her more wine. She covers the glass. "I have to pick up my nephew." Oh, nephew? So she's staying at her sister's. And she doesn't drink irresponsibly. She does text though.

I want the nephew to die but the woman to live. The shame worse than grief, worse than death. Sitting on that basement bed, a black dress, the evidence of wasted talent all around her, waiting until the last minute to leave, but needing to ride with her sister since her own car is obviously totaled. Why didn't she cover her brake while crossing that uncontrolled intersection? Where will she go now? She reacts to a noise off camera, though we hear nothing. She can't bring herself to move. She puts her hands to her knees to push herself up. Her back hurts.

Death, life, shame, grief. Wouldn't it be nice to write about something else?

Surely, I'll condense. Sculpture in the back seat. Open in the school parking lot. Fiery crash while checking texts. I want the nephew to die though. And I want her in that basement, in that dress.

# THE VOW

Once, like an idiot, I made a vow to be a better son. I was at my father-in-law's funeral, wrangling the kids during the depressing church-basement reception, surrounded by Atlee's red-nosed AA buddies, when it occurred to me that this would happen to my own parents soon. Relatively soon. Not that the idea is so unique, but at the *exact* moment I thought it Mary grabbed my sleeve and said, "You know it's nice that we moved near your parents. I wasn't sure it would be but I'm glad now. It's a comfort." We had recently moved back to my hometown, where I was now the high school football coach. Honestly, the hair on the back of my neck tingled when she said it—it was unlike her to grab my sleeve and blurt things like that out. And it was seriously at the exact moment I thought about my own parents' deaths. I also found it strange that she said, "It's a comfort," like a character in a book set in pioneer times.

I'll be honest, I pretty quickly ditched my vow. You get out of those church basements and life becomes much less dramatic. I never forgot; I just didn't do anything about it. Once a week I would think something like, *Shit, Dad might enjoy going on a bike ride right now.* Or *What if I text him and ask if he wants to get some ice cream?* (Apparently, I thought being a good son meant going out on dates with my dad.) Anyway, despite the many bike rides I went on and ice cream cones I ate, I never reached out to my dad unless I needed a favor—and even then, I would try to get Mary to text him. If my dad drank, maybe we could have perched on neighboring barstools and gotten silently drunk, though I suspect that is better in theory, and our fun, quiet, boozy evening would eventually devolve into marital confessions or affectionate declarations. No thank you.

My vow collected dust until just after school was let out for the summer. Mary needed the house to herself to study for her CFA Level 3 exam, so I took the kids to my parents' house to let them run around while I looked at my phone and ate snacks. The kids were out back with my mom, and I sat in the living room next to my dad, who, at two o'clock on this sunny Wednesday afternoon, was watching a movie on basic cable. I was surprised, considering the volume level, that our glasses of lemonade did not rattle against their coasters. He did not mute the commercials.

I hesitated to request a volume change, to keep intact our comfortable groove of interpersonal silence, but I soon had to admit to myself that I would rather chat than allow the deafening action-movie clatter to continue its assault on my eardrums. With heroic restraint, I politely and with feigned nonchalance asked him to please turn the TV down. However, he misheard me and thought I commented on the movie.

"You ever been there?" he asked.

Glancing over my phone, I attempted to convey disinterest, confusion, and annoyance using only my eyebrows. He must have taken the gesture as an answer in the negative.

"I've always wanted to go," he said. "The beaches look terrific."

Curious, I watched the movie until I recognized it as the updated version of *Miami Vice* starring Colin Farrell and Jamie Foxx.

"It's not difficult to go to Miami," I said. "You should just go."

"Tell that to your mother," he said. "Just try to get her to a beach."

I told him to go by himself. Nothing was stopping him.

"I can't," he said. "I get lost in new cities. Too many Spanish speakers there to ask directions. And besides, what can you do by yourself? I need someone around to remind me about sunblock and remember the name of our hotel."

I hesitated. Instinctively, I had a burning desire to point out the wrongness and ridiculousness of each of his reasons for not going to Miami alone. Suddenly, however, I recalled my vow. It seemed to appear before me and hover between me and my dad like a ghost, rendering me unable to explain to him how he's a grown man with a smartphone who can easily navigate his way around Miami.

I took a breath. "I mean, we could go."

"Oh!" he said, wagging his head as though embarrassed by a much-too-generous offer. "You don't need to do that."

I attempted to smile. "Seriously, I want to."

"You know, I think my days of wrangling children in strange cities might be over," he said, his eyes locked on the screen. "I love those kids, but it's too much stress."

I was aware that this was my last chance to bail. All I needed to do was shrug, slide my eyes back to this espn.com article previewing the upcoming NBA draft, sip my lemonade, and leave my vow simmering on the back burner. And yet I said, "No, what I meant was that you and I could do it. Go down for a long weekend. I'm sure it's cheap to fly there from Chicago. We could stay in an Airbnb. I can book everything."

Of course, he agreed, and I suddenly had this gigantic self-made hassle on my hands. Instead of relaxing and playing with my kids during my precious summer vacation, my waking hours would now be spent worrying about and planning for this trip. Not only that, but I had to explain to Mary that I was placing a problem in her lap by leaving for a couple days. And I couldn't even bag out of it because then I'd feel even *worse*. It dawned on me that I really screwed myself over with this vow.

My dad, I discovered only after we arrived in Miami, did not know how to use Google Maps on his phone. He wouldn't even try. I told him it was intuitive, that Google didn't want to trick him, that if he guessed at how it would work, he would probably get it to work. To this he would firmly shake his head and say that he only knew how to operate something called a Garmin, which is apparently a GPS maps device specifically for use in the car. He wouldn't even try to use Google Maps.

This meant that we had to go everywhere together. To the beach. To each meal. To eat an absurd amount of ice cream. He had all these tooth-gritting habits. Like how, whenever he saw a stranger reach out their phone to take a selfie, he would go up to them and ask if they'd prefer him to take the picture for them. While he did this, I would walk a significant distance away and pretend to be absorbed by my phone.

He also enjoyed talking to the service workers of restaurants and hotels that he did not patronize. He thought, because they smiled when he spoke to them, that they wanted to chat, and so he would ask them questions about the surrounding area and tell them where he was from and ask them personal questions and solicit entertainment recommendations. It never once occurred to him that he might be bothering them and wasting their time. The cheeriest I've ever seen my dad was when he was talking to hostesses of restaurants he did not go into.

I voiced these two complaints—about taking strangers' pictures and wasting the time of employees who were paid to be polite to everyone—over dinner the first night. He was thrilled to hear them. Apparently, he had no idea that bothering people was annoying. He said that he liked learning about himself and kept excitedly asking me if I had more complaints about his behavior. I did, but I didn't say so, and, reluctantly, I respected that he took my criticism so well. I certainly would not have reacted so affably. If he complained about my petty quirks, I would have melted into a teenaged fury and ruined our trip. I told him that I would keep him apprised of future grievances, though I was aware that I probably would not.

One complaint I kept to myself was about his eating habits. For instance, when we ate at a Spanish restaurant and he ordered paella, he said that he wanted to ask the waiter if they had soy sauce, because he had never eaten rice without soy sauce before. I told him in the most measured voice I could muster that this was a Spanish restaurant and soy sauce an East Asian condiment, that there was tons of salt and spices already in the paella, and to please not ask the waiter for soy sauce. Now it was his turn to sigh passive-aggressively, probably in response to my tone, but it was worth it because he didn't ask the waiter for the soy sauce. He only muttered, "It would taste better with soy sauce," and we finished our meal in silence. In retrospect I should have kept the mood light and let the soy sauce thing go, but the thought of him asking that waiter for soy sauce still makes my skin crawl. Many things about his dining habits bothered me—in addition to condiment usage, he asked the waiters for too much advice while ordering, he chewed and slurped loudly, and he used about a hundred napkins per meal. I kept all this to myself.

In bed at the Airbnb, I thought how the vow was ruining my life. Being a better son should have been a simple, natural undertaking. Perhaps the vow made me overthink it and, somehow, I had become an even worse son. Not to mention the havoc it wreaked upon other facets of my life. Mary was stuck home alone with the kids all day, I wasted all this money, and I was in Miami getting exasperated by my dad instead of at home lounging around with my own kids. If I were smart, I would have, right then, made a vow to break my original vow, but for some reason I could not bring myself to do it. That promise had a stranglehold. Just the thought of breaking it conjured the image of that churchbasement funeral reception. The dread it stoked within me surely meant there was a reason to keep to it.

The situation reminded me of that story about how things happen for unknown reasons—I tell it to my football team every season because it makes me sound wise and encourages them not to question my methods. The farmer in the story finds a horse and everyone says he's lucky, then his son breaks his leg trying to tame the horse and everyone says he's unlucky, then the army comes along taking all able-bodied young men to war, but the son gets out of it because of his broken leg and people say he's lucky again. Many things about that story confuse me, but I may have remembered it wrong. The takeaway, as far as the vow was concerned, was that maybe something lucky would happen to me soon. For the moment, though, I felt like a horseless man with a broken leg getting shot at in a trench.

Upon waking, I wondered how exactly I could bear another entire day with my father. Remarking on buildings, negotiating restaurants, policing his habits, putting sunscreen on his back. It was like a strange dream. If only he could use Google Maps.

We both had pretty bad sunburns, so we did not go to the beach. But what else is there to do in Miami with your dad? We walked around the city and kept asking each other if we wanted to go into different stores and buildings. The other person would always say, "Sure," and then we'd go in for a couple minutes and the person who made the suggestion would say, "Should we leave?" and the other would say, "Sure." Once, when we were, for no good reason, in the lobby of a fancy hotel, a man I had never seen before—a large, pink, smiling, ballcapped man with toggled sunglasses dangling from his neck—placed a hand on my shoulder, said my name, and asked if I was me. I told him I was.

"You're the one who doesn't punt, right?" this stranger said. "Who throws all the time and runs all those crazy plays?"

"Yep, that's him," my father said, putting his hand on my other shoulder.

It turns out this guy saw me give a talk at a coaching conference. I'm often asked to speak at these things because I employ a unique coaching system where my team never punts the ball away and always tries to score a touchdown. We also never kick field goals, always try onside kicks, run a lot of trick plays, and throw the ball almost every down. I didn't invent this system, some guy in Texas did, and I modified it with less-successful results, but my talks are still standing room only. Other coaches tell me that they want to employ this system, but as far as I know, nobody else does it other than me and that guy in Texas. It's risky because it bucks tradition, and if it doesn't work, you look stupid and will get fired, even though all the numbers and analytics back it up. But try to explain analytics to those old guys drinking coffee at the counter of the Milton Family Restaurant on Saturday mornings. Those are the guys who get you fired.

"So, how'd you guys turn out this season?" this guy in the lobby of this hotel asked.

"They lost their first four but then won their last five," my dad answered for me. "Almost made the playoffs. Without him they would have *stunk*."

The stranger smiled. He was obviously amused at my dad's pride in my barely above-average season.

"Well, now that is impressive," the pink man said.

The guy told me that he worked with the University of Miami football team. He gave me his card and said he ran a prestigious summer coaching clinic and that maybe there would be a place for me next year. He patted my shoulder and said to keep up the good work, and that he would watch out for news of my team. He spoke like he was doing me a favor, and implied that I should be grateful for his attention.

"You know who that was?" my dad said, still touching my shoulder despite my slight movements to shake it off. "Gus Robley!"

"The guy who used to coach Utah?" I asked.

"Yeah!" my dad said, his hand still on my shoulder.

"Didn't he get fired because of some sex stuff? With a cheerleader or student or team assistant or something?" I asked. I extracted the man's card from my pocket and confirmed that he was, indeed, Gus Robley.

"But man, he was a great coach. Was top ten a couple times over there—at Utah!" my dad said, ignoring the sex stuff. "And he recognized *you* straight off! Marveled at you! Beelined right up and put his hand on your shoulder! That Robley certainly has a presence."

Was this the time, in the horse story about how fortune is relevant and events happen for unknown reasons, that the townspeople would say that I was lucky? Because a creepy, washed-up college football coach with a past of sexual assault paid attention to me? Because from now on I might have to spend my summers at a coaching clinic, surrounded by

Gus Robleys, constantly worried that I was in over my head? I would rather break my leg.

I also had mixed feelings about my father's pride. On the one hand, it's good that my dad witnessed and fully appreciated the interaction. I had, after all, been complimented by a rather famous man who was an expert in my field. But it bothered me that my dad didn't seem to care about Gus Robley's ignominious past. He obviously thought that being a good football coach made up for being a bad person. I tried not to judge my father harshly because I had to spend the next twelve waking hours with him, plus an early-morning plane trip, and I was already full to bursting with grievances. I simply could have done without yet another reminder that my dad and Gus Robley were part of a generation of men who openly placed professional greatness above personal decency.

So I was feeling both lousy and a little gratified as we searched for a place to get lunch. My dad couldn't stop gushing about meeting Gus Robley and speculating about what the interaction might mean for my career.

"With Robley's help you could be a college coordinator one day," he said. "Maybe even a head coach at a small school. Could you imagine me and your mother coming to watch you in a real stadium?"

I didn't bother to explain that I was happy with my current low-pressure, smalltown coaching gig. I figured the Robley offer would never amount to anything. Old, high-profile coaches love to talk a big game.

We ended up going to a Cuban sandwich place. My dad ordered his with no pickles or ham. He also asked if he could have cheddar instead of Swiss cheese. And he asked if he could have ketchup instead of mustard.

While my dad, who was flabbergasted by the clerk's accent, was still leaning over the counter trying to properly amend his order, I got my food, found a table, and looked up on my phone why Gus Robley was fired from Utah. It turned out he had a long string of "student assistants" who personally accompanied him on trips and a couple years ago several came forward to blow the whistle about his inappropriate advances and the appalling ways he tried to keep them quiet. The thought of Gus Robley doing that to a college kid would make you sick. If you saw him, you'd especially know why. Maybe the grossest and most upsetting part of the story, though, was that Gus Robley was not fired because he tried to force people to have sex with him—that detail only came out later. No, he was fired because he illegally used school funds to pay for their travel and then used booster funds for hush money. He was caught after he got drunk and crashed his stupid motorcycle while one of these "assistants" rode on the back without a helmet. The student ended up in a coma while the helmeted Gus Robley walked away more or less unharmed. They fired him because of an accounting issue and now he's apparently employed by the University of Miami. Tell the farmer-and-horse story to that kid in her coma, see what she says.

I decided to impart all this Gus Robley information to my dad, to make him understand how misplaced his admiration was. But first I had to wait until after he successfully conveyed all his sandwich alterations, and then, through a series of questions, finally grasped the simple numbering system used for collecting his finished sandwich, and then tried to banter about the counter worker's coral necklace despite the rumbling and consternation of the growing line behind him. And then I had to wait while he searched for me with the head-cocking determination of a perched hawk hunting for prey, though I was about seven feet away holding my hand high in the air and loudly whispering, "Dad, Dad, Dad, Dad, Dad," and then, the moment he spotted me and relief spread over his face, someone called a number that I assumed was his, so I had to wait still longer while he collected his sandwich, bantered with the woman who handed it to him, and began his search for me anew.

The frustration that his ineptitude produced in me only strengthened my resolve to disabuse him of his admiration for Gus Robley. I was sick of these confident but useless old men, whose only desire was to run out the clock with as little complexity as possible, leaving us, the younger generation, to clean up their messes. The biggest problem was that their parochialism trickled down. Most of my idiot high school players also thought that a man should do what he wants and try his best not to get caught. And when I try to teach them otherwise, they simply stop listening to me because the right way isn't as fun.

So, vow or no vow, I was determined to summarize this 2014 *Deadspin* article about Gus Robley for my father. Maybe *then* he'd begin to realize how wrong his generation was about everything.

I had finished my lunch by the time he found the table again. This put me at an advantage since I wouldn't have to pause for bites in the middle of my Gus Robley story, whereas his mouth would constantly be full so he couldn't argue or tell me to stop. For some reason I was nervous, probably because my dad and I diligently avoid confrontation. My complaining about his behavior the first night of our trip was highly abnormal. I had been proud of myself for doing it, but also felt I had narrowly averted disaster.

To enhance the importance of what I was about to say, I looked him in the eyes. Apparently, I never do this, because I was shocked by his shriveled, frightened face. Thinking about it, I had never purposefully looked above his nose before. Though, especially during meals, I would often allow my gaze to linger on his mouth as I wondered how his chewing could reach such a volume or how the food particles spotting his cheeks could have strayed so far from his lips. But his eyes were something else entirely. They were vulnerable, anxious, hesitant. When our eye contact held, he smiled and nodded with far less enthusiasm than he would have for the maître d' of a restaurant where we didn't end up eating. The look he gave me should have been the one he reserved for strangers, not for his only son.

My resolve to explain the details of Gus Robley's improprieties faded fast. I'd gladly waste every summer for the rest of my life at that monster's coaching clinic if it meant I didn't have to endure this look from my father for an entire meal.

"What?" he asked while taking a huge bite of his sandwich.

"Have you always had that?" I asked, pointing at the corner of my own eye, near the temple, mirroring where I had, at the last second before being forced to speak, noticed a large bumpy mole on my father's face.

"Oh, no," he said, putting his head down and placing a finger near but not touching the growth. "It's just a skin tag."

It certainly wasn't a skin tag. He had those all over his back, as I had discovered during multiple sunscreen applications.

"I'm pretty sure that isn't a skin tag," I said. "Maybe it's a wart?"

"Yes, it could be," he said, obviously embarrassed about what was either a shameful wart or a cancerous tumor.

I could tell he didn't enjoy his sandwich after that. He chewed and swallowed with what appeared to be a dry mouth. I got up and poured him a glass of water.

As I waited for him to finish his meal, I wondered how much any of us know what we are doing. I didn't want to be in Miami. I was doing it so my dad would have a certain impression of me. I did this for no real reason—basically to satisfy an inexplicably made vow. If I told my dad how much I had dreaded making the trip and then how much I hated the trip itself, he would probably say, "Then why did you suggest it?" and I would have no answer for him. And yet I did these useless little life things constantly. I would continue doing them willingly. They involved planning and effort, and I had no good reason. Maybe sometimes a farmer can find a horse, and it's just a horse, and he can look at it and say, "Well, there's a horse; it's neither good nor bad, lucky nor unlucky. It's just a horse."

After lunch, my dad and I went out for ice cream.

Later that summer I fished for compliments from my mom about my good deed of taking my dad on vacation. This meant asking her if he had a good time but expecting that he had a great time and that my mom would praise me for the nice thing I had done. But my mom was coy and hummed her answers. She did not break her gaze from her laptop screen to elaborate on how good of a son I was.

"Wait, did he not have a good time?" I asked.

"No, he definitely did," she said, eyes still locked on Facebook. "He always enjoys spending time with you. And he *really* enjoyed meeting Gus Robley."

"What didn't he like?" I asked.

She hesitated and I pleaded with her. I told her it wasn't fair to keep such information to herself. I said, without believing a word, that underlying misunderstandings like these might one day fester, turn malignant, and ultimately prove fatal to my relationship with my dad, and that it would be entirely her fault if she did not properly warn me right now.

She sighed. "He just isn't comfortable away from home anymore. I think he mostly agreed to go to be polite. He said it seemed like you really wanted to go to Miami for some reason."

"Why would I want to go to Miami with Dad? I'd have to be insane. He said he wanted to go and so I said I'd take him. I was being *nice*. I never had any desire whatsoever to visit Miami before, especially with my own father." I spoke incredibly fast.

She finally turned away from her screen and faced me, on a roll now that she had the green light to be honest. "And he didn't like how you scowled at him when he talked to waiters."

It was a fair point about the waiters. I could have been more relaxed about that.

"But he liked the Gus Robley thing at least, right?" I asked, trying to salvage something.

"Oh, he *loved* meeting Gus Robley," she said.

Miami was a bust. After my conversation with my mom, I unofficially gave up trying to fulfill my vow, though it left me with the nagging feeling of an uncompleted chore. Like how once I left the storm windows up for so long that I didn't bother to take them down at all, since by then it was almost autumn anyway.

That season my football team figured out how to play the way I wanted them to. We won our first six games by an average of thirty-two points, which made my parents feel like big shots in our little town. During our winning streak, when I'd walk into their house, my father would mute the TV or put down the newspaper and call out, "There he is!" while my mom would flip down her laptop or rush in from the back garden, cup my cheeks, and beam.

The sudden uptick in their loving attention hurt a little. Apparently, they hadn't been enthusiastic about me until I began winning local football games. Not that I didn't accept their praise and consider my vow fulfilled, but now the victory seemed hollow since I fell into it ass backward. But what if we lost our last three games and missed the playoffs? I could only control so much. I couldn't throw or catch the ball. I couldn't tackle. I could only explain as best I could to my players where they should all be and what they should do when they are there. Winning football games was largely out of my hands.

The Saturday after our sixth win I went to pick up the kids at my parents' house—Mary was volunteering a shift at a women's shelter—and everyone came rushing out to greet me, even the kids. I think they picked up on my parents' newfound enthusiasm and wanted to join in. After my war hero's welcome, my parents sent the kids downstairs to play and each took one of my hands, pulled me over to the couch, and sat on each side of me.

"We have something we need to ask you."

"And he can say no. He can feel free to say no."

"But I can ask."

"You can, and I just want him to know that he can say no."

"But we'd both really like him to."

I clenched my entire body so hard that I began to shake.

They finally asked if I would go out to breakfast with them on Sunday mornings during the season.

"We want to show you off," my mom added.

"It can be a new family tradition," my dad added.

"Yeah, sure," I said, already lamenting my lost Sunday mornings. "The kids will love that."

"We were wondering"—my dad looked at my mom as if getting her permission to continue—"if it could just be the three of us."

"It's just more relaxing," my mom added.

First one and then the other, I looked at these crazy people, wondered how exactly their minds worked, and only then realized exactly what fulfilling my vow truly entailed, and that I had created an asphyxiating cyclone of affection from which I had no means of escape.

I closed my eyes and nodded.

Instead of taking the kids straight home I drove out to the country. My daughter loves cows. We pulled over on a dusty road overlooking a pasture and all three sat on the hood of the Subaru. A couple of the cows stared back at us warily, flicking their tails.

"Hooves!" my daughter yelled. It's what she always said when cows were in sight.

"Listen to me," I said seriously.

"Hooves!"

"Don't ever try to impress me," I told them. "You hear that? Don't even try to figure out how. Nothing you do will make me love you any more or less than I do right now, and I will only disappoint you if you expect too much from me. It'll be better for all of us in the end if you just live your lives. I'm only one man and, honestly, I don't know why I do half the things I do."

My daughter, Hannah, who is three, and treats Mary cruelly but is calculatedly sweet toward me, was already bored with the cows and slid off the hood to destroy some wildflowers. I nodded my approval. It seemed an appropriate response to my speech.

My son, Bruce, who is six, and inexplicably concerned with life's enigmas, furrowed his brow as he tried to parse what I had just said. His expression made me realize that one day soon he would nitpick my flaws in ways I can't possibly predict. Even if I did everything in my power to be a perfect father or to keep his expectations low, I was bound to fail him, and he was bound to resent me for my inability to recognize what I had done wrong. His troubled, pensive face continued to radiate confusion at what I had just said.

Or perhaps, I thought, young though he was, he understood that I was wrong and had bungled my attempt to let us both off the hook. Bruce's acute perception keyed in on the fact that, despite my desire not to, I expect to be enthralled by him so I can prove to other people how admirably I performed my job as a parent.

As though confirming my suspicion, he hopped off the hood of the car, carefully dusted himself off, and faced me.

"Dad, look at this!"

My son began mimicking a celebratory dance made famous by a professional football player. He crouched low and skipped along the country lane, staring out of his encircled fingers as though they were goggles or binoculars, and then he swung his arms like an ostentatious skier swishing back poles. After a few repetitions, he grinned and, with a rather maniacal nod in my direction, silently begged for my approval.

This flew in the face of my stated wishes, and yet hit the nail on the head. I was foolish to think I could compete against nature. So, I gave in, and mechanically clapped my hands in rhythm like a drugged participant at an obscure religious rite.

"Great dance, son," I intoned. "Great dance."

# Acknowledgments

The following stories have been previously published, and a number have been extensively revised: "Practice" in *The Southern Review* (as "Texting") and reprinted in *Coolest American Stories 2023*; "Petland" in *Southeast Review*; "Scorch the Earth Beneath Your Feet" in *Passages North* (as "Road Safety"); "At the Twin Pines Motel" in *Southern Humanities Review*; "Camera Lake" in *The Rupture* (as "Roofing"); "Ankle Grabber" in *Subtropics*; "Vultures" in *Painted Bride Quarterly*; "Props" in *jelly bucket*; "Wind" in *Jabberwock Review*; "Résumé" in *Green Mountains Review* (as "Road Crew"); "Pharaoh" in *Bayou Magazine* and reprinted in *Midwestern Gothic*.

ALEX PICKETT grew up in Wisconsin. He earned his MFA at the University of Florida and is the author of a novel, *The Restaurant Inspector*. He teaches creative writing at City Lit in London, where he lives with his partner, Elena, and their dog, Milo.